COUNTDOWN

TO DAWN

By Brett Hoeppner

THE EVENTS OF
ARMED INSTINCT...

The Vola Virus, a deadly disease that ravaged the world, ignited a second Civil War in the United States. Bio-Yomi, the world's leading medical technology company, developed an addictive cure for the virus referred to on the streets as "Vax." CEO and President of Bio-Yomi, Hirohiko Naito, leveraged his newfound power as the sole peddler of Vax worldwide to split the U.S. in two and claim half of it for himself as the Bio-Yomi Territories. He appointed his power-hungry daughter, Kimberly Naito, as head of the Red City branch of Bio-Yomi.

Grayson and Faith, two fearsome freedom fighters living in the run-down Red City, were shocked to discover that their young daughter had been kidnapped by Grayson's brother and delivered to Bio-Yomi for experimentation. With the help of their allies Kurt, Luden, and Dr. Sebastian Borka, Faith obtained a prototype flaming sword called Onibi and a battle-ready exosuit called Project Izanami. These weapons were powered by technology developed by Faith's father before he contracted the deadly Vola Virus while working for Bio-Yomi. With Grayson at her side, Faith used Onibi and Izanami to kill Bio-Yomi's half-human, half-cybernetic monstrosity called Steel Fist along with Kimberly Naito, resulting in the destruction of the Bio-Yomi Red City headquarters.

Grayson and Faith rescued their daughter and decided to lay low with Kurt in an abandoned Bio-Yomi bunker under a decrepit farmhouse outside of Red City. Luden used his role in the Red City battle with Bio-Yomi to rise through the ranks of his gang, The Psychophants, while Dr. Sebastian Borka was captured by Hirohiko Naito. Though Grayson and Faith lost a few limbs during their fierce battle with Bio-Yomi... at least they can live in peace with their daughter, Emily, once more...

Until the COUNTDOWN begins...

PROLOGUE
HEADS UP

The starry night sky above the desert outside of Red City whispered to the nocturnal creatures skittering to and from dying bushes littered across the landscape. The visible ribcage of a skinny coyote flexed back and forth as he darted after a fleeing rabbit, kicking up dirt and rocks in his wake. A deep explosion echoed in the distance, shaking the earth and causing the coyote to break stride and snap his head toward the noise.

A series of faint pops and guttural yelps sounded off from afar as the coyote looked back toward his lost prey, noticing it had vanished. He hung his head low and emitted a whine as his mate emerged from the darkness with the limp rabbit dangling from her jaws. Elated, the first coyote yipped and joined his mate as their paws pattered into the night, away from the violent commotion.

A smoking 9mm shell casing landed with a *ting* in the dirt next to the dusty combat boot adorning Luden's right foot. As blood trickled from his hairline and stained his black, cashmere turtleneck, he engaged the safety on his obsidian-colored Staccato 2011 pistol. Six bodies of armed men in cobbled-together tactical gear littered the ground as the headlights of Luden's overturned armored truck illuminated a crater in the middle of the dark, dirt road.

"Mother fuck…" Luden said as he rested a hand on his knee, catching his breath.

He focused his vision toward his overturned truck, its armored underside dented and cracked with a blast mark radiating toward its shredded tires. "PSYCHOPHANTS" was stylistically painted across the red finish on the side of the vehicle. A golden crown atop a laughing skull made up the letter "o."

"Is this going to happen to every fucking truck I get?" Luden cursed under his breath as he wiped a glob of blood and sweat from his forehead with the back of his hand.

Suddenly a *crack* echoed across the desert as a bullet landed between his feet and ricocheted with a trailing *kwang* into the night, leaving behind a puff of dust rising up to his crotch.

"Shit!" Luden exclaimed as he flinched and noticed a not-so-dispatched goon on the ground weakly pointing a pitted-out Glock 17 in his direction.

Luden disengaged his handgun's safety with a *click* and fired a shot that connected with the trigger-guard of the man's firearm. The bullet deformed the polymer trigger guard, ripped the man's trigger finger clean off, and sent the splintering gun flying from his now incomplete hand. The man let out a muffled shriek under his black gas mask as blood began to flow and fall from his finger.

Noticing his Staccato's slide was locked to the rear, Luden reached for a spare magazine while approaching the moaning and wriggling henchman. He fingered his empty mag-holder much to his chagrin.

"Well, I guess I lost that due to in-flight turbulence," he quipped to himself as he reached down and grabbed the wailing man by his foot.

Luden's broad shoulders flexed as he pulled the man in between his feet and sat down on his chest. Blood oozed from three gunshot wounds in the guy's abdomen as Luden's weight pressed down on his body, causing him to scream in agony under his mask. Luden patted down the thug's torn vest, ripped open a velcro pouch and removed a loaded magazine.

"I want to ask you some questions, but I can't hear a damn thing under that shit-filter on your face," Luden said to the man as he shucked five rounds into his hand from the recently acquired Glock magazine before discarding it.

The man mumbled something under his mask as Luden ejected his Staccato magazine, loaded the five rounds into it, inserted the mag, and chambered a round. Luden grabbed the man's gas mask and tilted his head to the side.

Pop, pop, pop!

Luden fired three rounds into the synthetic mask, flinging rubber and dirt across the ground. He pried into the mouth-area of the mask with his hand and tore open a ragged hole in the rubber. A garbled yelp emanated from the hole as blood drained from it.

"There we go!" Luden exhaustedly cheered, "First of all, who planted the damn bomb in the road? I've literally had that truck for, like, a week. I'd like some payback."

"Ga-blargah!" the man managed to eke out through his shredded, fleshy lips.

"Which one was Ga-blargah?" Luden asked as he peered at the five other bodies in the dirt.

"Well, doesn't matter anyway, I suppose," Luden concluded. "Next question! Who the *fuck* would be dumb enough to send you after the leader of the goddamn Psychophants? And I'd better hear you loud and fucking clear."

The vibrating roar of a motorcycle in the distance gradually crept into Luden's ears, growing louder with each passing second.

The desperate henchman took a wet breath. "Brazier…"

"Brazier?" Luden whispered in disbelief. "Fuck."

Luden reached for his belt, unsheathed a curved Bastinelli karambit knife, pierced it into the side of the thug's soft neck, and plucked out his carotid artery. He sheathed his knife and stood up as the man rolled onto his side, grasping his squirting neck. Blood rhythmically splashed into the dirt like a squirt-gun as Luden backed up toward his truck. He squinted as a single headlight grew larger and the rumbling of an engine grew louder.

The approaching motorcycle power-slid through the dirt and came to a stop fifteen-yards away from Luden, leaving a cloud of dust behind it. The rider revved the bike as he lifted a flamethrower over his head and released a stunning pyrotechnic blast of fire into the air. The light from the flame illuminated the bike, highlighting "Brazier" written in flaming letters across the gas tank.

Brazier, a bulky man dressed head-to-toe in stitched-together body armor, killed the engine of his motorcycle and planted his heavy boot into the dirt with a menacing *thud*. He wore a retrofitted firefighter's mask with thick bullet proof glass over his eyes and Kevlar shoddily stitched to the inside.

"Well, well," Brazier started with a gruff voice under his bullet-proof mask, "If it isn't Luden of the fucking Psychophants. You're a tough man ta ambush. Been tryin' to get at ya for weeks."

He rested his flamethrower over his shoulder as he casually moseyed closer to Luden. In his left hand, his thick, gloved fingers grasped a device similar to a harpoon gun with a red Torii gate symbol on the grip.

Luden leaned against his overturned truck, crossed his arms, and cracked a smile.

"And why does the loudest bounty hunter in Red City want to fuck with the leader of the largest gang in this Territory?"

Under the bullet-proof mask, Brazier's eyes lifted as he smirked.

"Let's—

Pop, pop!

Two puffs of dust floated off of Brazier's armored chest as Luden lowered his empty sidearm.

"What the fuck was that?" Brazier asked, clearly offended, as he shrugged his shoulders.

"So, it's really bullet proof, huh?" Luden inquired.

"Yes, it's really bullet proof. What the fuck did you think? You think I wear all this shit for fun?" Brazier responded, completely irritated.

"I don't know. I had two rounds left, I figured it was worth a shot."

"Well, are you fuckin' *satisfied?*"

Luden closed the slide on his Staccato and holstered it on his thigh.

"No... I wish it *wasn't* bullet proof."

"All right you little shit, you wanna fuck with me? How's this? Bio-Yomi is making fuckin' moves tonight. They're goin' after *you* and they're goin' after your *murderin'* and *thievin'* fuckin' friends. They hired *me* to get *you* 'cause they don't wanna start a fuckin' war with the Psychophants!" Brazier shouted, obviously spitting in his mask.

Luden froze in place.

"*Grayson...*" he worried under his breath.

"You know what, you chicken-shit mother fucker... shootin' me in the fuckin' chest... Take 'im dead or alive they tells me..."

Brazier pointed the harpoon-looking device off to the side, discharged it into the distance, and flipped a lever labeled "disconnect." A steel rope with a lassoed end rocketed into the abyss of the night. He dropped the device in the dirt with a *clang.*

"Oops. Well, I guess I have to deliver you to Naito in an urn instead, you piece of shit," Brazier yelled as he leveled his flamethrower at Luden.

A scorching blaze of fire careened toward Luden as he booked it and took cover around the opposite side of his truck. As flames violently crashed against the armored vehicle, Luden reached into the shattered rear driver's side window and began sifting through gun cases, ammo cans, and crates of supplies that had scattered throughout the interior.

"I'm gonna roast your philanderin' ass, Luden. My wife told me *all* about your little night together before I torched her, too! It's not every day you get a payday and pay*back* from the same corpse!"

On his knees, Luden desperately tossed aside more boxes in the vehicle as the heat of the flames licked the back of his neck. Suddenly, the inferno ceased and the flickering light from the flamethrower disappeared into darkness.

A bright orange, water-tight case fell directly in front of Luden from atop a pile of Vax containers. With haste, he pulled it out and plopped it onto the ground in front of him. The label on the front read: "Emergency Tool Kit, Smith and Wesson 500 Magnum." Luden popped the latches on the case, opened the lid, and gazed at the snub-nosed .50 caliber revolver nestled in pre-cut foam.

A sticky-note inside read:

Use in case of Steel Fist.

Ha-ha.

Happy Birthday, buddy.

-Kurt.

Brazier's heavy footfalls walloped the dirt as he rounded the side of the vehicle.

"I'm gonna piss on your charred corpse and watch it sizzle before I toss what's left of ya at Old Man Naito's feet," Brazier boasted.

Turning the corner, Brazier looked down the .50 caliber barrel of the .500 Smith and Wesson magnum revolver in Luden's hand, gasped, and ignited the pilot light on his flamethrower.

With a thunderous boom and a blinding muzzle flash, the recoil of the revolver cocked Luden's wrist toward the sky as his skin rippled from his forearm to his shoulder. The blast of raw energy leaving the muzzle of the hand-cannon blew Luden's hair back and rattled his teeth.

The massive five-hundred grain bullet punched Brazier in the chest. The Kevlar weave of his body armor caught the bullet, but stretched eight inches deep into his chest cavity. As the kinetic energy of the devastating bullet transferred into his body, it was as if a rope had been tied around his torso and attached to a fighter jet launching from an aircraft carrier. Brazier's dense body impacted the ground and limply somersaulted as a wall of dirt drifted across the headlights of the overturned truck.

"Holy *shit*. Grayson is going to be *so* jealous," Luden said, half-laughing.

Brazier, disoriented, got on his hands and knees and coughed blood into his mask. As the glass portion of his mask filled up like a red fishbowl, Luden picked up Brazier's flamethrower and ignited the pilot light.

"Looks like your *suit* was bullet proof, but *you* weren't," Luden wisecracked. "Tell me, Smartass, did you make your suit *fire*proof?"

All Brazier could do was choke on his own blood as Luden torched him like a forgotten marshmallow before tossing the flamethrower aside.

"Roasted at his own barbecue. You hate to see it," Luden joked as he turned away from the burning Brazier and hopped onto his motorcycle.

With a roar of the engine, Luden revved the throttle, looked down at the harpoon-like lasso gun in the dirt, and focused for a moment on the Bio-Yomi logo on the grip.

"Don't worry, Emily. Uncle Luden's coming."

Luden peeled out in the dirt, hopped up onto the road, and thundered into the night as the crackle of Brazier's fiery body filled the emptiness of the desert.

CHAPTER 1

CRITICAL STRIKE

"**D**ammit, Kurt! I told you, I can't do it!" Faith angrily cried.

Faith dropped her wooden katana on the floor and the sound of its impact echoed through the makeshift dojo in the underground bunker beneath the abandoned barn.

"Come on, now, Faith. It just takes some good ol' fashioned hard work. You'll get the hang of it," Kurt said as he clicked the heels of his mechanical prosthetic legs together, causing his belly to jiggle a bit.

Faith collapsed to the ground and pounded her carbon fiber prosthetic arms against her matching prosthetic legs. She looked up at Kurt with a deadened glare.

"I knew what I was doing when I climbed into that Izanami suit. Why can't any of you just leave me alone? I can't protect her anymore... That's just the way it is," she admitted.

"Mommy!" a tiny voice shouted from behind her.

Little Emily with her shining black hair in a ponytail ran to Faith and jumped into her lap. Faith's black gym shorts and white tank top wrinkled and twisted as Emily gave her a big hug.

"Hello, my darling," Faith responded with saddened hesitation as she loosely embraced her.

Faith reached down and tugged on her daughter's beaded, friendship bracelet that read, "Emily."

"This is already getting to be too tight on you… You're growing so fast," Faith pointed out with a hint of melancholy lingering in her voice.

Grayson stood in the doorway and clanked his metallic left arm against the steel door frame.

"So… How was it today?" he awkwardly asked.

Kurt playfully punched a practice dummy with a drawn-on angry face, then approached Grayson. He ran his hand across his greasy apron and sighed through his white, bushy beard.

"It's uh…" Kurt started cheerfully before trailing into a more despondent tone under his breath, "It's been six months, Grayson. I can only help her along so far. But, if she doesn't *want* to improve, then there's nothing I can do for her. Those arms and legs have enough power to swing the sword and move around. But they can't do it on their own."

"Emily, baby," Grayson shouted in an uplifting voice.

"Yeah, daddy?" she responded with glee.

"Why don't you go with Kurt into the cafeteria to get a quick bedtime snack."

"Really, I can?" Emily replied with genuine surprise as she jumped out of Faith's lap and stood at attention.

"I'm sure we can find you something very yummy, Emily! Come on now," Kurt said with a smile as he motioned for Emily to join him.

Emily ran over to Kurt and placed her tiny hand in his as they moved past Grayson and out of the room.

Grayson closed the steel door behind him and flanked Faith who still sat on the floor.

"What's the matter with you, Faith? This isn't like you..." Grayson asked, suppressing his frustration.

Faith inspected the metallic fingers on her hand as she raised and lowered them one at a time.

"I had the dream again last night, Gray. I'm in the Izanami suit... And I move Onibi closer and closer to Kimberly Naito's face. Right as the heat from the flames on the sword start to melt her skin... She turns into Emily. And no matter how much I scream or how hard I fight... I can't stop my arm. And I watch her as she slowly burns alive," Faith explained as she stared through the practice dummy, "But this time, she said something right before she died."

Grayson stood over Faith and glanced at the dummy's angry face.

"What'd she say?" Grayson asked.

"Just one word," Faith answered, "Father."

"Dammit, Faith. It's just a dream. You have to snap out of this... *thing* you're going through. Someday, Bio-Yomi could come for her and *you* have to be strong enough to stop them again," Grayson pleaded as he reached down, placed his hands under Faith's arms, and stood her up.

"And why does it have to be *me*, Grayson? Huh? Why me? I've done my part, I got our daughter back, I even saved *you*... I've got nothing left, Gray. I'm a shell of who I used to be. I feel empty."

"It *has* to be you! What fucking good was I? I..." Grayson paused to fight the quiver in his lip, "I failed our daughter, Faith. I couldn't save her. I gave it *everything* I had and it wasn't good enough. Emily needs *you*. I need you. You have to pull it together. If not for me, or for you... then for her."

Faith's eyes welled up as tears trickled down her cheeks.

"It's not just a matter of *pulling it together*, Grayson! I should be fucking *dead*! Look at me! *Look* at me!" she screamed as she horrifically examined all four of her mechanical limbs.

"Faith... I'm..." Grayson started to say after taking a breath.

Suddenly a muffled boom sounded off overhead as the room forcefully shook, throwing the two of them off balance and knocking over the training dummy. Their eyes immediately met.

"Those were the tripwires in the barn," Grayson said, eyes wide in disbelief.

"Shit... Grayson, I'm not ready for this... I can't..."

"Come on, we've got to get out of here. If that's *them*, we won't stand a chance like this..." Grayson interrupted as he scooped Faith into his arms and sprinted out of the room.

With watery eyes, Faith stared over Grayson's shoulder at the useless wooden sword she had left behind until they turned the corner and he continued to carry her down the hallway of the bunker. Grayson kicked open a steel door and saw Emily hugging her knees in the back of a utility van as Kurt hurriedly loaded equipment into it.

"Out the back door?" Grayson asked as he gently sat Faith on a nearby metal table.

"I saw the camera feed before they killed it... Bio-Yomi's got a damn army out front. Hell, we'll be lucky to make it out the back. I've just about got everything we *absolutely* need packed up, but we've got to get the hell out of here," Kurt said breathlessly as he motioned to Emily sitting in the van leaning against a shiny, windowed capsule containing Faith's Izanami battle suit. He continued to frantically load cases and crates into the van, grunting as he heaved them with all his strength.

Tears gently pelted Faith's robotic legs as she sat on the table with strands of her long hair draped over her face. Her eyes despondently wandered across the room, pausing on Emily in the van, then on Grayson and Kurt worriedly discussing a plan. Helpless pangs squeezed her chest as her vision settled on her sword, Onibi, resting on the table next to her. She admired the intricacy of the katana blade that was crafted for her mother and then stared deeply into the pulsing, blue biomagnetic energy source that swirled in the chassis near the grip of the weapon.

"How the fuck did they find us, Kurt? We are in a bunker no one knows about, under a barn, in the middle of fucking nowhere. You estimated *years,* not *months* before they found us. God *dammit.* Come on Faith let's…" Grayson began to say as he heaved an enormous rifle into the back of the van.

As he looked toward the table where he had set Faith, his heart instantly sank when he realized she was gone. The lights in the bunker cut to pitch black before a red backup light dimly lit up the room. Without a second thought, Grayson lifted the front of his white t-shirt, reached into the waistband of his black jeans, placed his hand on his concealed sidearm and took a step toward the door.

Grayson felt a firm squeeze on his bicep followed by a forceful tug. He turned and looked directly into Kurt's eyes who had just grabbed him.

"Grayson, we are *out of time.* If anyone has a *right* to make their own decisions… it's *Faith.* One way or another, she'll be okay. But right goddamn now, they are after your daughter and we need to get her the hell out of here. You are her *only* chance," Kurt lectured with burning eyes.

Grayson glared through the red light toward the door Faith had left ajar, fighting his one-track mind. He clenched his jaw, released the grip of his handgun, and approached Emily as Kurt released his arm.

"Alright, baby girl, you hang on tight back here and I promise I'll keep you safe," Grayson reassured Emily with his hand on her cheek.

"Where's Mommy?" Emily asked, shivering with fear.

"She's coming, Em. Your mom's a superhero, remember?" Grayson said as he comforted her, forcing a wink of confidence.

Emily nodded and buried her head in her arms as Kurt shut the double-doors on the back of the van. Grayson ran to the driver's door and climbed in as Kurt hoisted himself into the passenger seat.

Grayson started the ignition and shifted the van into drive. The yellow headlights shined down a dark and seemingly endless underground tunnel as he pressed on the accelerator. Both Kurt and Grayson stared at the side mirrors of the van, praying to catch a glimpse of Faith in the reflection as they disappeared into the shadowy tunnel.

Outside, rain began to trickle onto the splinters of the demolished barn in the muddy field above the bunker. Ten white SUVs outfitted with mounted miniguns rested silently in the downpour guarding a single armored personnel carrier with red Torii gate decals on each side of the vehicle. Bio-Yomi soldiers outfitted in black, tactical gear sat patiently still in the vehicles, waiting for any sign of movement.

A soldier sitting in the driver's seat of an SUV flinched as mud splattered onto his windshield.

"*Jesus.* He scared the fuck out of me," the soldier spouted, hitting the windshield wiper lever as his comrades smirked at him.

Standing in front of the SUV was a shirtless man towering seven feet tall in a mechanical, battle-ready exosuit accented with red, glowing lights. His wet, midnight hair stuck to his shoulders as his perfect, chiseled physique glistened in the rain. Glowing red tubes with shielded, titanium coverings ran from an armored plate in the center of his chest, along his neck, back, arms, and legs. His tank-like, yet sleek, exosuit outlined his entire body, covering all of his extremities except for his chest and head. The fluorescent paint from the Bio-Yomi Torii gate symbols on the exosuit's pauldrons shimmered as the man's bright-red, synthetic eyes flared in the night.

"How many did we lose in the blast?" the handsome man in the exosuit asked with a reverberating voice.

"We lost a team of five, Sir," a soldier's voice answered in his head via radio communication.

"Insignificant," the man stated coldly.

"We are ready to proceed now that you've arrived. Lead the way, Sir," the soldier informed him over comms.

"For Kimberly," the man said with conviction as he activated his exosuit and took a forceful step forward in the mud.

Suddenly, a fiery blue blaze kindled in the night as Faith ignited Onibi and held it at her side. The sapphire flames of her sword flickered across her body as the light rain in the night began to soak her lengthy, black hair causing it to stick to the back of her tank top.

"Holy fucking shit, it's Faith!" a Bio-Yomi soldier screamed over comms.

Every SUV door sprung open as the fear-stricken soldiers took up defensive positions and trained their rifles on her.

Faith's chest heaved with bated breath as the flames of Onibi licked her face and reflected in her dead eyes.

The handsome man's face lit up in the exosuit with a blood lusting passion as his mouth contorted into a primal grin.

"I have been waiting for this moment for six months. Come at me, FAITH!" the man's reverberating voice pierced through the rain.

The man flexed the hand of his exosuit, causing a five-foot long, double-sided machete with pulsing, red edges to extend from his arm. As the handle hit his robotic hand, he gripped it with a sharp *clank* and zoomed toward Faith with blinding speed, leaving a laser-like trail in his wake.

"Die!" he commanded in a vicious rage as he reached Faith and swung the hulking weapon toward her.

"Hiroya!" a calm, but powerful voice shouted from behind the man.

The blade stopped just short of Faith's neck. The laser-edge of the massive machete seared a few wet hairs near her cheek, causing a puff of sizzling smoke to drift through the breeze.

"But, Father! She…" the man in the exosuit began to protest.

"Step aside, Hiroya! She is no danger to anyone. Are you? Young lady?" the voice boomed.

As Hiroya removed the blade from Faith's neck and stepped aside, Faith noticed the door to the armored personnel carrier had opened and a figure in a gray suit was approaching in the dark. She released the trigger on Onibi's chassis, killing the flames before she loosened the grip of her prosthetic hand, dropping the sword in the mud.

"So fierce when you murdered my unarmed daughter, but so helpless in the face of the men of the Naito family," Hirohiko Naito observed with authority as he came face-to-face with Faith.

"Just, get it over with. Emily is long gone," Faith stated with an undertone of self-loathing.

The pits and wrinkles in Mr. Naito's face compressed a bit as the hint of a smile teased the corner of his mouth.

"Your effort to distract us is wasted, I'm afraid. I am not here for Emily. In fact, my men have orders to kill your husband and Mr. Kurt Duncan should they cross paths... but I have ordered them to leave your daughter alive and alone. She is innocent of your sins. I am a *reasonable* man, after all," Mr. Naito continued with an ominous authority, "My son was ordered to make you submit to capture, which I must say was much easier than I foresaw. I mistook you for a ruthless killer, but you have shown yourself to instead be an opportunistic coward."

Faith dropped to her knees causing mud to splatter her bionic legs. Through a veil of her wet hair, Faith shamefully looked into Mr. Naito's eyes

"I killed your daughter in the most painful and gruesome way I could. So vile, that I can't get her death out of my head. I've killed hundreds of people without a second thought, but her death was so inhumane that it *haunts me*. She took *my* daughter and I'd kill her a thousand times again for that. Each time more horrific than the last. If you are such a reasonable man... then you have to see, past your grief, the *reason* in my actions."

Hiroya scoffed as his blade re-sheathed into his arm and he turned his back. Mr. Naito knelt down to Faith's level and tilted his head, staring deep into her soul.

"And as a parent, you have to understand why I will cause you the most painful and prolonged death that the creative scientists and engineers of my company can possibly imagine... Regardless of my daughter's actions, you murdered my child," Mr. Naito retorted with pure, looming supremacy.

Rapid footsteps squished in the mud as a soldier approached Mr. Naito.

"Sir, Alpha team has intercepted and is engaging the secondary targets," the soldier announced before a distant crackling of gunfire erupted in the distance.

Panic washed over Faith's face. Her heavy heartbeat consumed her body as she felt a momentary jolt of strength return to her arm. It no longer felt like a prosthetic arm, it felt *real*.

Mr. Naito turned to look at the soldier, still kneeling in front of Faith.

"Excellent, tel—"

Faith wrapped her fingers around Onibi's hilt and, with one swift motion, ignited the flaming blade and sliced clean through Mr. Naito's torso from his hip to his shoulder. She released a desperate scream as her hand weakened, releasing the lever on the hilt, and extinguishing the flame.

The bottom half of Mr. Naito's silver tie fell to the slimy ground as he stood up and looked down at Faith, seemingly unharmed by the devastating attack.

"You cut my favorite suit," he said as he turned to walk back to the APC, "Hiroya… Take her."

"No!" Faith desperately screamed as the gunfire in the distance slowed down before ceasing altogether, "*How…* how did you…"

Mr. Naito paused and half-turned his head toward Faith.

"I have the most influence of any man in the world. I cured the world populace of the deadliest virus in human history. Every major country is addicted to *my* vaccine and will pay anything… perform *any favor* for it. I've hired the best scientists in the world in every field, the best engineers, the top experts in cybernetics, the best doctors and surgeons… I have an infinite supply of currency. I am the worldwide monopoly on technology. Did you *really* think I wouldn't find a different path to immortality? *This* is why I do not need your daughter. If you must know, I do not even know if I can kill her. She is either immortal, or just a key to immortality. Regardless, I have the rest of eternity to deal with her. And she will have until then to feel the helpless pain of being the sole reason for her parents' deaths."

Faith balled her artificial fingers into a fist and sat her on heels in defeat.

"So, it was all for nothing?" She asked, dejected. "How did you find us?"

Halfway back to the Bio-Yomi vehicles, Mr. Naito raised his voice to respond.

"It is a… happy side effect… of my power. I can sense biomagnetic energy."

Mr. Naito turned his foot sideways to half-face toward Faith.

"I sensed the energy in your sword and my daughter's Izanami suit you stole… but another source has been floating around this area. Your acquaintance, Sebastian Borka, tells me it is most likely an 'echo' of the other sources based on its erratic movement. But it is a frustrating nuisance for me, like a mosquito buzzing around my ear. You wouldn't happen to have a third source, would you?" Mr. Naito genuinely asked, letting his commanding presence falter for a moment.

After a long pause of silence, as Faith sat motionless in the rain, Mr. Naito closed his eyes, massaged his temple, and motioned toward his son before climbing into the armored vehicle. Hiroya approached Faith, retrieved her sword, and spat on her head before grabbing a fistful of her hair and dragging her toward the vehicles.

Faith catatonically stared into the starry sky as raindrops pecked her face and mud caked onto her body. The previously fearful soldiers joked and snickered at Faith as they re-entered their vehicles and closed the doors with a nearly simultaneous *thump*.

Chapter 2

I NEED A HERO

"It's coming up! The exit is one-hundred feet after the green light!" Kurt barked in the passenger seat of the van as it rocketed through the nearly pitch-black tunnel.

Dull, red lights on the ceiling hypnotically passed overhead as Grayson tightened his rough hands on the steering wheel.

"Daddy, I'm scared!" Emily shouted from the back of the van.

"It's okay, Emily! I'm not letting anyone take you ever again. Daddy's going to get you out of here," Grayson firmly told her before glancing worriedly at Kurt.

Kurt's aged eyes observed Grayson for a moment before he reached toward the floorboards and retrieved a bulky Tavor TS12 bullpup shotgun with one hand and a short-barreled, tactically outfitted AK-47 with a 75-round drum with his other.

"Green light's coming up, Grayson. Take your pick," Kurt said, tapping his fingers on the firearms.

"Pass over the AK. I know you are more of a scattergun guy," Grayson answered as he reached out and retrieved the AK-47 from Kurt and laid it in his lap.

"Fast or slow?" Kurt asked as a wave of green light flashed through the cab of the van from above.

Grayson glanced over his shoulder at Emily, who was shivering with fear in between two stacks of containers in the back.

"We're going slow. I want to go as cautiously and carefully as possible. Can't risk cowboy-ing it. Not anymore…"

The tunnel behind them lit up red from the van's brake lights as Grayson slowed the vehicle to a gentle stop a few feet away from a small ramp leading to a large garage door.

"Slow and steady, then," Kurt confirmed under his breath as he retrieved a remote from the glove compartment and pressed the button with his callused thumb.

Metal wheels squeaked in the tracks of the heavy garage door as it slowly lifted from the ground revealing a cloudy night sky above. Grayson killed the headlights and slowly accelerated up the ramp.

In the eerie silence of the night, Grayson and Kurt could only hear their heartbeats as the van climbed the incline. As the front end peaked and exited the tunnel, a sprinkle of raindrops pattered the hood of the vehicle. The front end leveled out and the view out the windshield transformed from the dark, misty sky to a shadowy, verdant field.

A flash of blinding light painted Grayson and Kurt's faces as their hands instinctively shielded their eyes.

"Fuck!" Grayson managed to curse before he popped the van into reverse.

"Oh, God," Kurt mumbled in fear.

An earthquake and a shockwave of dust blew past the van as Grayson watched an explosive charge detonate on top of the tunnel, collapsing the exit behind them. Emily screamed, covered her ears, and squeezed her eyes shut in the rear of the van.

"No, no, no," Grayson desperately repeated as he put the van into drive and wrapped his right hand around the pistol grip of the short AK-47 in his lap.

The blinding light ceased as the spotlight that was facing them faded to darkness. Grayson could make out two sets of headlights in front of them. He reached for the lever near the steering wheel and turned his own headlights back on.

Two Bio-Yomi SUVs with manned, rooftop-mounted miniguns were pointed directly at them. An additional eight soldiers armed with rifles stood in a half-circle around the front end of their van.

A single Bio-Yomi goon that Grayson hadn't noticed emerged from the group holding a two-tone CZ-85 Combat handgun at his side and approached the van with confidence. He was dressed differently from the other soldiers, wearing a red beret and gray-camo fatigues with a black plate-carrier on his chest, indicating he was a Bio-Yomi officer.

"Grayson! Kurt! Out of the car slowly or I will have my men cut your van in half," the officer ordered with a frightening air of seriousness.

Grayson's heart beat faster as his eyes darted everywhere looking for a way out. His hand twitched, almost raising his AK-47 up to the windshield to engage the soldiers before his survival instincts blocked him from doing so.

Kurt's hand began to tremble on the grip of his Tavor shotgun despite his calm, but sweaty, demeanor.

"You're not taking young Emily from us again, you hear?" Kurt shouted through the windshield as his slick palm tightened on the shotgun.

Emily's lips quivered as she pressed her hands harder against her ears.

"Fuck, Kurt. What do we do? Our backs are to the *fucking wall* here. I don't… I don't think I can shoot my way out of this…" Grayson muttered to Kurt as he continued surveying his surroundings.

"Grayson, hearing those words come out of your mouth officially has me shittin' in my britches. If *you* don't think you can shoot your way out of something, then I know we are truly fucked, my friend…" Kurt replied before exhaling through tight lips.

"We're not here for the girl," the officer shouted to Grayson, "I couldn't give a fuck less about her. I want *you*! So, both of you get the fuck out of that vehicle *now* or I'll have that whole fucking van turned into scrap metal!"

Kurt sighed. "You ever been captured before?" he asked while flashing a skeptical look at Grayson.

"Nope, this'll be a first. But what fucking choice do we have?" Grayson said before turning to meet eyes with Emily. "Em, no matter what happens... Just know your Mom's gonna come for you. You know why, right honey?"

Tears trickled down Emily's face as she got on her knees and sat on her heels.

"Sh- She's a superhero, Daddy," she answered through a quivering lip before sniffling away her tears.

"That's right, Emily," Grayson said with praise, "You stay right there, okay? Don't look outside and be sure to cover your ears."

Emily nodded despite her fear, covered her ears, and closed her eyes as she pressed her back against a pile of crates and slid down to her butt.

"What do you figure our odds are, Grayson?" Kurt asked frankly, trepidation in his eyes.

"Oh, I figure about one percent if we pop out guns blazing and make for the trees. Two percent if we surrender," Grayson responded matter-of-factly.

Kurt clanked his metallic knees together and let out his signature jovial laugh.

"One percent is pretty generous... But so is two percent... Well, hell, Grayson. I suppose two's better than one, then?" Kurt assumed, lowering his shotgun to the floor of the cab.

"Last chance, Grayson!" The officer spat with fury as he raised his hand.

Grayson exhaled and tossed his AK-47 onto the dashboard.

"Faith, I hope you're out there..." Grayson whispered to himself.

They both opened their doors and exited the vehicle. Their feet smooshed into the mud outside as they squinted from the sprinkling rain.

"In front of the vehicle, now!" the officer yelled, raising his sidearm toward Grayson.

Grayson smirked and shook his head at the faux-tough guy ordering him around as he and Kurt walked in front of the grill of their van.

"Now on your fucking knees!" the officer ordered as he anemically roundhouse kicked the back of Grayson's knee.

The officer nearly lost his balance as his boot bounced off of Grayson's leg. Grayson furrowed his brow as he looked at the man in disbelief.

"On your knees or I'll shoot your fucking teeth out," the officer threatened, his voice beginning to shake as he pressed the muzzle of his CZ-85 against Grayson's mouth.

The urge to forcefully snatch the handgun out of the man's grasp jolted through Grayson's body, but he resisted and got on his knees one leg at a time. Kurt fell to his knees with his eyes locked on Grayson ready to follow his lead.

The officer placed his hands behind his back and began to pace with a shit-eating grin adorning his face.

"Grayson. The Gray Ghost… You are a very feared man, you know that? Not as feared as your wife after the last trip you guys took to the Bio-Yomi Red City Headquarters, though. Hell, most of these men are too scared to even say her name," the officer chuckled, "Say, where is dear wifey? She didn't… split off from the group, did she?"

Grayson and Kurt worriedly flashed a glance at each other as the officer stopped and bent over at the waist to face them.

"You see, Mr. Naito can sense these things. The main force was focused on *her*. We are here to exterminate the rats who ran out the back," the officer continued, "The fearsome *Gray Ghost* didn't even put up a fight. I knew, deep down, you were a pathetic coward. While your wife slaughtered all of our men six months ago, she did it face-to-face… With a fucking *samurai sword*. Now *that's* impressive. But, *you*, the fucking *coward*, stabbed my younger brother in the neck from behind with a fucking *pocket knife* while he was on his break atop the guard tower. Then, like the coward you are, you sniped all of our men from a distance… just like you did on Vax Day."

The officer looked over the top of Grayson's head, smiled, and flapped his fingers in a waving motion.

"And now *I* get to kill the infamous information broker of Red City along with the Gray Ghost. And your daughter gets a front row seat in the splash zone of the show, Grayson," the officer explained as he clicked the button on the radio mounted to his vest, "Primary, this is Alpha. Inform Naito that we've intercepted his *pests*, over."

Grayson and Kurt glanced behind them to see Emily peering down at them through the windshield. Grayson snapped his head back to the officer only to look down the barrel of the 9mm handgun pointing directly into his left eye.

"Roger that, Alpha. Over and out," a crackling voice responded over the radio.

A heavy, metallic *thump* echoed behind the officer, originating from one of the SUVs. The officer took a step back from Grayson and turned to face the Bio-Yomi vehicles. The man on the minigun mounted to the SUV on the left was missing.

The Bio-Yomi soldiers glanced around confused when, suddenly, the man behind the minigun mounted on the other SUV fell limp, thumped his helmet on the roof of the car and disappeared into the sun roof of the vehicle.

"Did you hear anything? *See* anything?" The officer shouted at the soldiers.

"The fuck is going on?" A soldier asked as he dropped to a knee and looked around.

"Over th—" A soldier began to shout before his right eye liquified like an oozing, puss-filled pimple and his body fell lifelessly into the muddy grass.

"I didn't hear a fucking shot!" Another soldier shouted as they all took cover around their vehicles.

"Sir, get down!" A soldier shouted to the officer from behind the wheel well of one of the SUVs.

The officer squinted into the pitch-black night as he slowly walked away from Grayson and Kurt. His eyes grew wide as a line of bright headlights, belonging to six vehicles, flicked on a couple hundred feet away from them. The engines of the vehicles roared as their wheels kicked up mud and they careened toward the soldiers.

"Over there!" the officer pointed, "Open fir—"

The officer heard a distinct spring-loaded *shuck* behind him before a heavy impact punched the side of his neck. Then he felt a smooth tug as warm wetness washed down his flank and a steady drip pelted his vest. Strong, vice-like fingers gripped his shoulder and spun him around as he found himself nose-to-nose with Grayson.

"Boo," Grayson whispered as he retracted the blade of his black, Microtech switchblade in front of the officer's face.

The officer, petrified with horror, loosened his grip on his pistol as Grayson placed the knife into his pocket and backed away. The CZ-85 sunk into the mud as blood flowed onto it, painting the two-tone finish completely red before his body smacked into the wet earth next to it.

"Hop on the mini!" a soldier hollered.

"*Shoot those fuckers!*" another ordered, pointing at the approaching vehicles.

An eruption of gunfire rang out as muzzle flashes flared from behind the two Bio-Yomi vehicles. Grayson and Kurt sprinted away from the booming reports and toward the cab of their van as a soldier climbed on top of one of the SUVs, taking hold of the minigun's controls.

Bullet fragments sparked off of the approaching vehicles, lighting them up enough for the soldiers to identify that they were heavily armored and painted with red and white Psychophants colors.

As the soldier on the minigun hit the firing button and the barrels began to spin, a massive armored vehicle smashed into the side of the SUV flipping it into the air as a torrent of bullets discharged with a *brrrrt* into the sky. Soldiers who had taken cover behind the vehicle were knocked over and they scrambled to make their way back up to their feet from the slippery ground.

The SUV crashed into the mud and rolled, cutting the man on the minigun in half and flinging his torso into a nearby tree.

Another armored vehicle collided with the remaining SUV and knocked it over onto its side as the remaining vehicles slid to a halt in the mud. The doors all popped open as Psychophants gang members emerged and unleashed a torrent of automatic fire on the remaining Bio-Yomi soldiers. Puffs of ceramic dust exploded from the soldiers' body armor and chunks of flesh and blood peeled from their faces, necks, arms, and legs as a wall of bullets impacted their bodies.

"No stragglers, no stragglers!" a Psychophant bellowed from one of the vehicles.

Two soldiers sprinted from the wreckage toward Grayson's van until Grayson and Kurt emerged from the cab with their weapons in hand.

Grayson released a burst of fire from his short-barreled AK-47 that lit up his face with a ferocious and concussive muzzle blast. Three 7.62x39mm rounds connected with the nearest soldier's neck, chin, and nose, opening his face like a bloody baked potato and sending a cascade of fleshy blood pouring down his chest. His knees collapsed and his body stiffly impacted the wet soil.

Kurt discharged his twelve-gauge bullpup shotgun and the significant recoil rocked his weight onto his back foot. The one-ounce slug entered the second soldier's right eyebrow, punched through his skull and impacted the inside of his helmet. The chin strap of the soldier's helmet snapped, breaking his jaw, as the helmet flew out of sight like a punted football. Bits of skull fragments and brain littered the ground behind him as his heavy corpse plopped into the grass and thick mud began to fill his empty head.

"I think I just blew that guy's mind," Kurt chuckled as he rested the butt-pad of the shotgun on his hip.

Grayson's head swiveled left to right like a turret as he inspected the area for additional threats. Seeing only Psychophants gang members outfitted in outlandish post-apocalyptic garb stripping Bio-Yomi soldiers of their gear, he reached into the cab of the van and scooped Emily into his arm, holding her tight.

"You're okay, Emily... You're okay..." Grayson repeated as he placed his chin on her shoulder and held her tight.

"Daddy, what did you do to those men?" Emily innocently asked, her voice wavering with anxiety.

He set Emily on the ground and her white tennis shoes sunk into the dark, mushy mud.

"Daddy had to hurt those men because they were going to hurt daddy," Grayson explained, kneeling down to her level.

"Okay..." Emily quietly replied, rubbing away the dried streams of tears on her cheeks.

Emerging from the darkness, Luden appeared in the headlights of the van and patted Kurt on the shoulder. He rested a .22 caliber Henry lever action rifle with an attached SilencerCo Switchback suppressor over his shoulder.

"Come on, you're glad to see me," Luden suggested to Grayson with a grin across his face.

"Uncle Luden!" Emily called out as she took off through the mud toward him.

She crashed into his leg and held it tight as he ruffled her hair.

"Hey there, Kiddo!" Luden said, greeting her as he looked up to Grayson and Kurt.

"Listen guys, pleasantries aside, we've got to move. Bio-Yomi's got a whole army back at the barn and we don't want to bump into them on the way out of here. Follow us back to base and we can try to make sense of all of this," Luden explained before peeling Emily off of his leg, patting her back, and nudging her toward Grayson.

Grayson looked through the trees toward the direction of the barn and the bunker while obsessively rubbing his fingers with his thumb.

"It would be suicide, Grayson. I sent a scout that way and he's telling me some frightening shit going on over there. If it'll get you to move, Faith's alive. But if we don't go now... Well... *We* won't be," Luden illustrated, leveling with him.

Luden casually held his rimfire lever action rifle at his side, the blued receiver glinting in the headlights of the van.

"Slice!" Luden called out toward the Psychophants still rummaging through the Bio-Yomi gear.

A skinny young man with a tuft of hair on his chin jogged up to Luden.

"Think you can still act like a Bio-boy?" Luden asked as he glanced at the dead officer laying in the mud.

"I'm on it, boss," Slice responded quickly, eager to please.

Grayson hoisted Emily into the van, held her cheek for a moment and smiled at her.

"That was good work on those minigun assholes, Luden. Open sights and everything. I told you that 'can' was quiet as hell," Kurt complimented Luden, pointing at the silencer as Slice picked up the radio from the officer's vest.

"Thanks, man. You spoil me," Luden replied with a wink.

"I spoil you because you are as loyal as they come, my friend... It also helps that you happen to be my best customer," Kurt responded, stroking his shaggy beard.

"Alpha reporting, targets down. Got messy as expected. We'll clean up here and report back at o-three hundred, over," Slice expertly reported over the radio.

"Roger that, Alpha. Must be one helluva mess. Give Grayson's body some extra love for me. Primary out," the radio crackled as Slice tossed it to the ground, gave Luden a thumbs up, and headed back toward the armored Psychophant caravan.

"These *fuckers*..." Luden sneered under his breath, taking aim at the dead officer's head with his rifle.

With only the *click* of the hammer falling, a puff of gas exited the end of the silencer and a .22 caliber hole emerged in the officer's skull. A chunk of scalp peeled off like a flap as Luden cycled the lever action, ejecting a tiny shell casing into the mud.

"Not like you to get so emotional, Luden," Kurt mentioned as he grabbed hold of the handle on the inside of the van's cab, ready to hoist himself in.

"Yeah... Bastards wrecked my truck," Luden lamented as he tossed the rifle over his shoulder once more and took a step toward his caravan.

"Again? You had that thing for a week!" Kurt shouted before closing the door and resting his shotgun on the floorboards.

Luden waved him off, then whistled for his men while pointing to the sky and circling his hand.

"Where are we going, Daddy? Is Mommy there?" Emily asked, sitting on Grayson's lap.

Grayson put the van in drive and exhaled as his heart began to slow down and his adrenal glands stopped pulsing.

"We're going somewhere safe. Now climb in the back and hide behind the crates again, okay?" Grayson instructed, pinching her chin.

"Okay, Daddy," Emily exhaustedly complied as she climbed into the back.

Kurt glanced over at Grayson and smirked.

"You owe him now, you know…" Kurt said, egging him on.

"Yeah, yeah…" Grayson muttered as he cranked the steering wheel.

As the caravan of armored Psychophant vehicles pulled away from the carnage they had unleashed on Bio-Yomi, Grayson pressed his foot into the accelerator and followed the string of tail lights in front of him.

Chapter 3

LOST AND FOUND

Faith's body slammed into a white, tile wall, sending a spider web of cracks across it. Hiroya, with the shiny black hand of his exosuit, reached down and gripped Faith's head. He lifted her off of the ground and peered into her eye between his fingers.

Behind him was a partially lit room with flickering lights and steel tables topped off with discarded lab equipment. Twelve Bio-Yomi soldiers watched the interaction with victorious smiles and bated anticipation creeping across their faces.

"To think… a warrior as fierce as you has lost her fire. I envisioned a heavenly battle with you before striking you down in front of Father. You were the motivation behind this… *permanent* alteration to my body. If I didn't have further use for it beyond fighting you, I might have regretted the excruciating pain I endured to obtain this power," Hiroya pontificated with a hint of muted heroism, "But… That pain was nothing compared to the pain of losing Kim… Seeing you *torture* her on video…"

Hiroya gave Faith's head a restrained squeeze, eliciting no response from her. He opened his hand and watched as she rag-dolled to the floor. With a quick shove from his robotic foot, Faith slid across the ground and hit the wall once more. She sat with her back against the cracked tile as she blankly stared at the glowing red tubes on Hiroya's glistening chest.

"I'll let you say hello to your old friend before we begin enacting our karmic justice on you for the pain you've caused all of us," Hiroya said as his reverberating voice penetrated Faith's ears.

He motioned toward the guard closest to the double doors at the back of the room. The guard pushed the door open with the buttstock of his rifle as a thin man in a wheelchair sheepishly rolled into the room. The thin man's veiny neck flexed as he shamefully struggled to raise his head to look at Faith.

Faith's eyes darted over to the man who was missing his right leg up to his knee and his left leg to his thigh. Two disfigured hands, with three remaining fingers each, quivered beneath the white sleeves of a lab coat. The face of the man had an eye patch over the right eye under a pair of spherical glasses along with a missing right ear. As Faith focused on the man's trembling lower lip, she recognized him to be a severely mutilated Dr. Sebastian Borka.

"*I'm sorry…*" Borka mouthed to Faith as she closed her eyes in grief.

Borka turned in his wheelchair and started to slowly exit the room. Hiroya smirked at Faith before turning to catch up with Borka.

"Soldiers! You were all handpicked based on closest relation to the victims of the Red City terrorist attack on Bio-Yomi R&D. Thirty minutes, and make sure she survives. Or else you'll have to deal with my father," Hiroya announced as he walked past the soldiers who began taking off their helmets and gloves.

Hiroya ducked through the doorway in his mechanized suit and began speaking to Borka as they rounded the corner.

"I'm returning to Capital HQ. I retrieved the missing asset and tossed his corpse in the basement. Pick him clean of any Bio-Yomi tech he might have, then dispose of him. I want this facility—" Hiroya ordered as the door closed behind him and the heavy *thumps* of his footsteps trailed off.

"My best friend," said a soldier as he revealed shoulder-length blond hair from under his helmet.

"My brother," a gruff soldier with a buzz cut sounded off as he tossed his glove onto a table.

"*My* brother," another soldier's muffled voice grumbled under a balaclava.

"My son…" an older, balding soldier squeaked out through tortured sorrow.

Faith's eyes slowly panned the room looking for her sword, but came up short. As she realized there was no way out, she closed her eyes and prayed for a painless death.

Her eyes shot open with excruciating pain as she gripped her right hip with her prosthetic arm and let out a guttural scream.

"Ohhh! Looks like you can feel that after all!" the blond soldier yelled as he jolted her robotic leg with a device reminiscent of a large electric prod.

The rest of the men, anxious to have their turn, closed in as the soldier with a buzz cut kicked her in the side of the head. Another soldier knelt down and punched her in the stomach with his bare hand, knocking the wind out of her and making her fall onto the ground in the fetal position.

"Fucking bitch," he said, spitting on her chest.

"How much of you is real, after all, huh?" the blond man taunted.

He pressed the switch on the prod and electrocuted her left breast, causing her to scream like a wounded animal. Faith beat her head on the hard floor as tears streamed down her face and mixed with her blood on the crumbling tile.

She tried to stand up, but lost control of her legs and fell to the ground once more. The twelve soldiers in the room rowdily cheered him on as they reveled in her pain.

"Look at her fucking *go*! *Bzzt, bzzt*! Not so fucking tough now, *are you*? Fucking coward *bitch*!" the blond soldier said as he moved the prod toward her once more.

Suddenly a thunderous *wooshing* noise whipped across the room with the wind-pressure of a helicopter's rotor blade. An ornate odachi, a massive katana with a 5-foot blade, crashed into the floor and stuck straight up, vibrating gently.

The blond man's hand fell from his wrist, still grasping the electric prod.

"What the…" the man started to say before glancing at his missing appendage, "FUCK! MY FU- HAN—"

The soldier started to hyperventilate as an overwhelming volume of blood fell from his cleanly severed wrist, painting the floor.

"What in the *fuck?*" the soldier with a buzz cut exclaimed as the soldiers' eyes grew wide in disbelief.

The dim lights in the room began to flicker faster as the colossal odachi mystically lifted from the floor before flying to the back of the room.

A tall man wearing head-to-toe white-colored samurai armor with a faded red, metallic Tengu mask caught the sword by its enormous handle and stood at the ready in front of the double doors at the back of the room. His intimidating mask featured a long nose, bushy eyebrows, a thin moustache, and smiling demonic teeth.

Through the windows of the double doors behind him, the hallway on the other side had been completely drenched with blood.

"*Goddammit!* Quick, don't let hi—" the older soldier began to scream as he scrambled for the rifle he had set on a nearby table.

The samurai flicked his wrist, sending the odachi flying like a spear toward the man. The lengthy blade pierced the older man's body, swept him off his feet, and pinned him to the back wall. The samurai made a pulling motion with his hand and the sword unsheathed itself from the wall and the man's body. As the soldier slid down the wall, the samurai made a sweeping motion, causing the odachi to swiftly decapitate the man across the room and effortlessly cut the wall deeply in the process. An arterial spurt of blood from the man's neck splattered across the ceiling as the headless body crashed to the ground next to Faith.

"Dear god…" the recently handless blond man said as he witnessed the inhuman horror that had taken place in front of him.

The great sword returned to the samurai after he beckoned it back to his hand. The group of soldiers in the room began drawing pistols from their holsters, scrambling away, or running for their rifles. The samurai slowly walked toward Faith as he, seemingly telepathically, manipulated the gargantuan katana throughout the room, chopping the remaining soldiers into leaky bits and pieces. Body parts flung across the room as if they were run through a wood chipper, and lines of blood and shredded clothing splattered across the walls. A thick, red wave rippled across the floor as the room began to flood with gore.

With a wave of his hand, the odachi cleanly cleaved diagonally through the blond man. As the top half of the blond soldier's body slid off of his legs, the heavy sword quickly cut it into three more halves before it hit the ground. A bucket's worth of blood smacked the floor in tandem with the body's giblets as the cumbersome sword whipped around the room like a deadly piece of shrapnel in a tornado.

Maintaining his slow walk, the samurai tilted his head down and held his fist to his chest, holding up his index and middle finger close to his heart, seeming to focus harder on the control of his sword.

With a final slash, the blade sliced the soldier with the buzz cut across his waist. The samurai reached out and choked the man's neck as he kicked his lower half away. The soldier's guts and organs splashed to the ground as his intestines dangled like wind chimes.

"Please…" the man managed to squeak.

The furious eyes of the samurai's Tengu mask stared fiercely at the soldier until the tip of the sword poked through from the back of the man's head and out his mouth. His severed tongue stuck onto the sword like a kabob.

The tip of the odachi removed itself from the man's head as the samurai tossed what remained of the soldier's limp body onto a nearby table. The samurai whipped his arm out to his side and the odachi flung the tongue and a streak of blood onto the wall in front of him. The tongue slowly slid down the wall as the samurai beckoned the odachi back to him. The sword floated around his body, then stuck to his back like a magnet.

Step by step, the towering samurai walked through a lake of warm blood, kicking away chunks of meaty flesh until he reached Faith, who had propped herself up against the wall.

She looked deep into the maddened eyes chiseled into the steel Tengu mask as the samurai bent over and reached his hand out toward her.

With a confident, but strained voice the samurai calmy called out through his mask, "Take my hand, Cherry Blossom."

"Dad?" Faith murmured, her eyes widening and then welling up with tears.

Faith deeply sobbed, planted one of her prosthetic feet in the ground and stood up on her own. She crashed into the samurai's chest, wrapping her robotic arms around him, as she cried deeply into the armored plate hanging from his neck.

With a bit of hesitation, he wrapped one arm around her shoulders and placed his other hand on the back of her head, pulling her close.

"I know… I'm here," he replied with a muffled voice as a single tear traveled beneath his mask and down his neck.

Chapter 4

SILENT NIGHT

Grayson checked on Emily over his shoulder and saw that she was sound asleep in the back of the van, gently bobbing with the motion of the road.

"We're approaching the gates," Kurt said with his arms crossed in the passenger seat.

Brake lights on the vehicles in the caravan lit up as they approached an enormous, rusted, and armored gate with "PSYCHOPHANTS" painted across it. On either side of the gate were towering walls with spikes lining the edges and automated turrets peeking over the top. It was crude, but well-constructed with top-notch technology protecting it.

Steam ejected from the center of the gate as the vault-like locking mechanism engaged and retracted before it opened like a door made for giants.

As the caravan entered car by car, Grayson and Kurt looked around the makeshift, but impressive city residing inside the walls. Weapons vendors, gunsmiths, food stands, and peddlers advertising Vax lined a marketplace in the center of the sizeable camp as a group of teenagers were shooting at pop-up targets in front of a berm of dirt nearby. Families holding hands walked through the market, a cluster of children threw knives in the dirt at each other's feet, and an old man twirling a revolver in his hand stared at Grayson as he drove by.

"This isn't what I expected... Looks like everyone, even the kids here, are addicted to Vax. That shit turns you into a night owl. I guess that explains the liveliness," Grayson mentioned as he followed the directions of a man waving his hand toward a spot to park with the rest of the Psychophants vehicles.

"Yeah, Luden's my number one purchaser of Vax. It's a damn shame. To think, not a single person has weaned off of Vax without dying... When the Civil War was brewing, these poor people were forced to pick between trusting a corporation or trusting a Government. Too bad the game was rigged. They lost either way," Kurt responded, "Luden told me about this place. Excelsior, they call it. It's a nomad-type city free from the rule of Bio-Yomi in the middle of this damned desert. Kind of ironic that they took an abandoned Government terraforming project and turned it into their home."

"Well, it certainly looks... free..." Grayson complimented with his tongue in his cheek.

"It's rough around the edges, but I don't think you realize how big of a fucking deal it is that we are in here right now," Kurt emphasized, "Nobody, and I mean *nobody*, that isn't a Psychophant has ever made it past that gate."

Grayson put the van in park, turned off the ignition, and exited the vehicle slamming the door behind him. As he surveyed the hand-built city with shacks and huts made out of scrap, he noticed people pointing at him and muttering to each other.

"Luden, how in the hell did you end up in charge of all this?" Grayson mumbled to himself as he opened the rear-doors of the van.

Inside the vehicle, Emily stretched and yawned before standing up and shuffling over to Grayson, who scooped her into his arms.

"Daddy, is Mommy here?" Emily pried once more, beginning to worry.

Grayson watched as Luden reached into one of the Psychophants vehicles and slipped on a merlot-colored duster with a colorful laughing skull wearing an ornate crown stitched onto the back of it. Luden then muttered some orders to his men and rushed to a steel, elevated stage with "PSYCHOPHANTS" spelled out in forged scrap behind it.

Luden stomped on a pedal on the stage and bright pyrotechnics exploded from behind the scrap-built "PSYCHOPHANTS." Women in dusty robes, men with spiked jackets, and children with graphic t-shirts depicting skulls and weapons gathered around the stage as Luden wrapped his hand around an ornate microphone.

"Citizens of Excelsior! Tonight, Bio-Yomi has declared war on the Psychophants! You might be seeing a few new faces around town, but *fear not!*" Luden triumphantly shouted into the microphone as his voice resounded throughout the entire settlement.

He stomped on the pedal again and flames erupted from the stage once more. His voice echoed through the speakers mounted across the encampment.

"We have, on our team, the fearsome *Gray Ghost*, the living legend who single-handedly took down every vaccine distribution spot in Red City on Vax Day," Luden bragged as he motioned toward Grayson.

People in the crowd began to gossip and point at Grayson as a few guys in the crowd nodded at him.

"Tonight, is the first night of our future! Tonight, is the night that we make our first move against Bio-Yomi! Tonight, we take the first step toward taking our cities back from the corporate overlords who poisoned our people! And tonight, We the People, say *NO* to Bio-Yomi! Just like We the People said NO to the Government that failed to represent us years ago!" Luden preached into the microphone, "Tonight, we go to *war*! And when Psychophants go to war… PSYCHOPHANTS WIN THE FUCKING WAR!"

Throughout the scrapyard of a small city, people cheered and began firing weapons over the walls. Luden, hyped up in the moment, kicked over the microphone and jumped off of the stage, running toward a group of armed Psychophant men to give them orders. Emily clapped in Grayson's arms with her mouth wide open in amazement.

"What did I just watch?" Grayson asked, perplexed by Luden's out-of-character display.

"Hey, I've never seen him like that either. Only heard stories. I'll be damned," Kurt responded as he reached into the van and began unloading crates.

Grayson set Emily down next to him and started to help Kurt unload his equipment.

Luden jogged up to them, removing his maroon duster on the way.

"I'm a little embarrassed you guys saw that..." Luden admitted as he caught his breath and uncomfortably scratched the back of his head.

"Luden, I knew you took over the Psychophants. I also knew the Psychophants were the largest gang in the Territory... But this is a damn *city*. Look around, you might as well be mayor of Gun Town," Grayson said in utter disbelief.

"Yeah, well, we're gonna need a lot of guns if we're going to counter-punch Bio-Yomi. So, there are worse places to be mayor of..." Luden replied, half joking.

Kurt grunted and set another crate down on the ground.

"What's uh... What's up with..." Kurt hesitantly mentioned pointing to the duster in Luden's hand.

Luden, flustered, began to stammer.

"Yeah... It's tradition for the leader of Excelsior and the Psychophants to have some flair. I have big plans for our future... But, uh... one step at a time..." Luden explained, blushing a bit.

"Luden," Kurt reassured him with a calming tone, "You'll always be the tactical turtle neck guy to me."

Luden chuckled before dropping his grin and touching Grayson on the shoulder, turning him away from Emily.

"Listen, my scouts tell me that Bio-Yomi got ahold of Faith at the bunker. They had to break their tail, but the last they saw… they were headed to Capital City," Luden quietly informed Grayson and Kurt.

Kurt closed his eyes, his heart broken, as he took a moment of silence. Grayson, without pause, reached into the back of the van and removed his go-bag.

"Then I'm loading up and going to Capital City right the fuck now. Can you keep Emily safe here while I go after Faith?" Grayson forcefully stated with complete focus as he tossed his bag over his shoulder.

"Yes, we've got a school here in a bunker with armed guards where they can protect her. But we need to be smart about this—" Luden began to suggest.

"*Fuck* being smart, I'm getting my wife back. I need a car and some more guns," Grayson ordered, his tone growing aggressive.

"I'm coming with you Grayson," Kurt said as he popped the lid on a container revealing a surplus of ammunition.

"Guys, listen to me—" Luden began to say before he was cut off by one of his men.

"*Contact*! Bird in the sky!"

Grayson, Kurt, and Luden looked to the sky and saw a black, unmarked helicopter silently descending into the main square of Excelsior.

Luden snapped into action, pulled out a smart phone, and expertly moved his thumbs on the screen. An alarm began to sound throughout the city as its citizens ran to shelter. The automated turrets all spun around and locked on to the helicopter.

"Goddamn Ghost Chopper," Kurt muttered, "Never thought I'd see one. That's post-split Government technology. Might be the only one in existence."

Suddenly, the alarm ceased and all of the automated turrets powered down.

"RPG, *firing*!" a bulky Psychophant with a mohawk shouted as he pointed an RPG-7 at the chopper.

A backblast exploded from the launcher as the rocket zoomed toward the helicopter. As it was about to impact the chopper's flank, the rocket stopped dead in its tracks and fell to the ground, completely inert. The man who fired the rocket lowered the launcher and stared with his mouth agape.

Grayson picked up Emily and set her in the back of the van.

"Stay in here, Em. And don't move for a bit, okay?"

"Yes, Daddy," Emily responded unsure of what was going on as Grayson closed the doors.

Luden, Grayson, and Kurt approached the helicopter as it noiselessly landed in the square.

The side door of the helicopter slid open and an athletic man wearing a crocodile-skin cowboy hat, a black dress shirt, a designer leather jacket, black slacks, and crocodile cowboy boots confidently stepped out of the helicopter. The eerily soundless propeller blades slowed to a stop as the man adjusted a large, silver belt buckle with a mini .22 caliber North American Arms revolver ornamenting it. He reached into a bag of gummy worms in his hand and popped one into his mouth.

"Luden! Been a long time, man!" the mysterious man announced as he chewed the gummy worm with an open mouth.

"Should we be worried?" Kurt directed at Luden as Grayson stood by, placing his hand under his shirt and gripping his concealed Heckler and Koch USP 9mm.

"This… is Rio. He was my CIA contact before the Civil War went hot," Luden flatly explained.

"You had a CIA contact? When you were contracting?" Grayson asked, genuinely surprised.

Luden waved at his armed men who had surrounded the chopper to stand down.

"I had a CIA contact because I had a cousin in the CIA," Luden answered, shaking his head and pinching the bridge of his nose.

Rio held out his arms after he bit the head off of another gummy worm.

"Whaddya think, Luden? Dressed for the Territories, huh! Blend in with the locals?" Rio shouted as he spun around.

"You look like a fucking tool," Luden insulted before turning to Kurt and Grayson, "This guy was the only fucking member of my family that sided with the U.S. Government. The rest of us stayed out here. Dangerous freedom over peaceful slavery we said... Unlike this phony patriot."

Rio stuffed his gummy worms into his jacket pocket as he approached Luden.

"No slavery for me, cousin. I'm at the top of the food chain, so I do whatever the fuck I want. Plus, you're about to be really fucking glad I stayed with the Government. You got a more comfortable place we can talk? For real, this is serious shit, Lu," Rio said, dropping his jokester persona.

Grayson relaxed his posture and hurried back over to the van to retrieve Emily. Kurt, completely intrigued, visually studied the helicopter.

"Sure, step into my office," Luden offered, motioning toward the improvised city, "What about your pilot? He coming?"

"Nah, he's picking up his wife and they are going to an open house in New York. Then he's coming back to get me. This is all off the books. He just... owes me..." Rio responded, with a shit eating grin.

"Things are pretty cushy in the New United States, aren't they?" Luden implied disapprovingly.

"Yeah, well... We keep it cushy for the loyalists so they don't ask questions. They're too afraid of hearing any answers that might inconvenience them," Rio responded as if Luden expected that answer.

Luden turned to walk toward the scrap-laden buildings of Excelsior.

"Might as well have called yourselves the *Old* United States. Nothing's fucking changed," Luden called out over his shoulder.

Rio took in a deep breath of air as he looked at the people of Excelsior going about their night.

"Yeah, it hasn't changed a bit," Rio parroted with a hint of longing trailing from his voice.

As the helicopter noiselessly lifted off and disappeared into the night sky, Grayson, now with Emily on his shoulders, caught up to the group. He, Kurt, and Rio followed Luden into the heart of Excelsior, passing groups of gawking onlookers along the way.

CHAPTER 5

RUNNING WITH THE DEVIL

"The Gray Ghost, in the flesh. Fuckin' wartime celebrity right here," Rio gushed, pointing his thumb at Grayson as he plopped onto a torn-up leather couch.

Luden waved goodbye to Emily as she held the hand of a pleasant-looking woman and walked down the hallway. He then closed a heavy, steel door behind him and heaved a large, sliding lock into place, securing the door behind them. Kurt and Grayson sat on stools surrounding a pool table with a map of the region sprawled across it. Red City rested on one end of the map, Capital City was on the other end, and Excelsior was smack-dab in between them.

"I've never felt so conflicted about a man in my life, you know? You fight with Bio-Yomi against the U.S. Government, kick their ass, and then turn around and kick Bio-Yomi's ass. I'm not sure if I should kill you or kiss you!" Rio jested as he pulled out his package of gummy worms again.

"I never fought for Bio-Yomi. I fought for a free America. And once Bio-Yomi turned on freedom, I turned on them," Grayson affirmed with a chilling seriousness.

"Hot damn! Grayson! Look at my arm! You gave me goosebumps!" Rio exclaimed as he rolled up the sleeve of his leather jacket, revealing that he did, in fact, have goosebumps.

Kurt, disgusted by Rio's sleaziness, swiveled his stool around and inspected the nearby map.

Luden walked across his office that looked more like a weapons museum than a place of work. Pistols, rifles, and shotguns of all makes and models lined the walls and rested on tables. He walked behind his vintage wooden desk and draped his Psychophant duster over the back of a torn-up, leather office chair before sitting in it. He moved aside a black Jericho 941 R handgun and a stainless-steel Wilson Combat 1911 pistol on his desk. Resting his elbows on the warped wood of the desk's surface, he made a triangle with his hands and rested it under his nose.

"Rio, you violated Bio-Yomi airspace at the risk of being shot down and tortured. Not to mention, you risked re-igniting a deadly war that neither side can afford to fight. *Why?*" Luden queried as the heel of his black, combat boot tapped the concrete floor.

Rio crinkled the bag of gummy worms into the couch cushion behind him and licked his fingers.

"We've wasted enough time as-is, so I'll just rip the hooker's shorts and get to work. What we have here is a little thing the Government calls a *situation*. I call it, *the end of fucking times*," Rio warned as he leaned forward, making the couch squeak as his weight shifted, "Hirohiko Naito A.K.A. the head of Bio-Yomi, A.K.A. the most influential man in the world, A.K.A. father of a dead daughter, has achieved *immortality*. Or, at least from the evidence we have collected, *invulnerability*."

Luden glanced over to Grayson and Kurt whose expressions fell with discontent. Kurt sat in silence as Grayson's brow twitched.

"That's not possible, he needed Emily to do that..." Grayson mentioned, challenging Rio's assertion.

"Did he?" Rio asked, "Or is that what Kimberly Naito *thought*?"

"No, he couldn't have done it without her. I'm sure of it," Kurt punctuated with a hesitant certainty.

"Kurt Duncan. Former smart guy for Bio-Yomi. Currently the number one information broker in Red City. Come on, Kurt. If anyone could figure this out, it would be you," Rio jibed, encouraging Kurt to put the pieces together.

"It's just... not possible," Kurt reassured the group.

"Kurt, Kurt, Kurt, my good man! How does the saying go? Denial isn't just a river in Egypt anymore? Denial, The Nile... Beside the point... Answer me this, *how* did your good partner Bryan discover the groundwork for the biomagnetic energy source?" Rio prodded.

"It's impossible, Bio-Yomi didn't know. There were no others. Impossible," Kurt responded, crossing his arms.

"I'll ask the question again, Kurt. We don't have a lot of time and you are being the monkey in the wrench, here," Rio countered with growing frustration.

"Answer him Kurt," Luden said from behind his desk.

Kurt sighed and shook his head, as he struggled to piece things together in his head.

"Well, what do I have to lose at this point?" Kurt asked, taking a deep breath. "When Bryan lived in Japan and was working at Bio-Yomi before they relocated to the States, he was part of a deep-dive discovery team that journeyed to unfathomable depths in the ocean floor. As far as I know, the U.S. still doesn't have the technology we were using decades ago. Bryan discovered a new species of fish. He called it the Glowing Dynoclast on account of the fact that it glowed blue…"

"Bryan is Faith's father, right?" Luden interrupted, starting to put the bigger picture together.

"That's right. Long story short, he and the fish ended up in my lab where we discovered that the fish was glowing blue because it was infected with an undiscovered parasite. After further experimentation, the fish couldn't be harmed. Damn thing healed instantaneously. Cut the fish in half, it seemed to reverse the wound. The whole damn world was lucky that Bryan discovered the fish and I discovered the parasite, because we may have been the only two men at Bio-Yomi who were willing to bury the damn thing to stop humankind from unearthing immorality," Kurt explained as he relived the past and searched for its relevance in current events.

"Did Faith know this?" Luden asked, leaning back in his chair with a look of worry reflecting from his eyes.

"Far as I know, Bryan never told *anyone*. I mean, hell, he would have used the damn thing to save his wife if we hadn't gotten rid of it for good," Kurt replied.

"And *how* did you 'get rid of it for good?'" Rio asked as a crooked smile crept across his face.

"Well, we didn't want to completely squander the discovery. So, we cloned the parasite a few times, dissected it, reverse engineered its biology, and used it to make the biomagnetic energy source. Turned potential immortality into a powerful, alternative, potentially infinite source of energy. Then we destroyed the parasites, and erased all data on the fish and the parasite. We claimed we invented the energy source together from scratch. End of story. But, it's impossible for Naito to *use* any of that information let alone *know* it. Bryan combed the surrounding area of the ocean for an additional year and never found even a *trace* of another parasite. It was a fluke, a freak of nature," Kurt asserted with finality.

"I have to stop you there... Bio-Yomi can *clone* living things?" Grayson asked, blown away by the information.

"Only living things that fit in the device. So, if you have a hamster you want cloned, feel free to stop on by. Wouldn't even fit the fish, that's why we just cloned the parasite. It was a big-ass parasite, though..." Kurt clarified.

Rio scooched to the edge of the couch and spread his hands wide, ready to drop a bomb.

"Well, Kurt, in the interest of time, let's cut to the chase. Remember Sebastian Borka? Your intern at the time? Guy who replaced you at Bio-Yomi? Yeah, well it seems he was craftier with tech than you thought, because he managed to retrieve the raw data on the clone of the parasite at some point. Turns out it was a bit corrupted, but still fairly intact. He was finally able to reverse-engineer it himself just recently... That is... After Naito tortured him for a few months and gave him a team of the best damn scientists in the world. And now, *voila*! Hirohiko Naito is an invincible man on a mission to dominate the world. Hot DAMN, don't corporate and government secrets get you fucking *HOT*!?" Rio shouted as he clapped his hands together with excitement.

"Luden, you trust this whack-job? How do you know all of this?" Kurt probed them, visibly offended and suspicious.

"Let's just say, a very knowledgeable ghost popped up and reached out to the New U.S. Government for help. Wise move if you ask me..." Rio said, placing his hands on the back of his head and leaning back into the couch.

Kurt's mechanical legs whirred as he shot out of his stool and lunged at Rio. Grayson caught him at the last second and held him back.

"Goddammit, nobody else knew that! Who's your source? Who told you all of that?" Kurt spat as his fury popped a vein in his forehead.

"Oh, the info-broker is *jealous*! I've told you enough, for now. But, as you can imagine, the New United States isn't thrilled with the idea of Hirohiko Naito obtaining invulnerability. He is allied with every major country in the world with the exception of the New U.S. Based on our surveillance, he is setting up an extravagant reveal of his newfound power for tomorrow. Now, Kurt, if you can control yourself for a moment... One final question. How did you destroy those *invulnerable* parasites?" Rio asked again as he tried to work a stuck piece of gummy worm loose from in between his teeth.

Kurt caught his breath and shook Grayson off of him. A wave of shock washed over him as he finally put it all together.

"We had to destroy every single one of their cells simultaneously. If even a single cell survived, the entire parasite would regenerate..." Kurt answered in despair.

Rio launched off of the couch and flamboyantly pointed at Kurt.

"Ding, ding, ding! We have a winner! That's why at 6:00 a.m. tomorrow morning, the New United States will be launching a pre-emptive nuclear strike directly on top of Hirohiko Naito," Rio explained, actually excited by the action.

Grayson stormed over to a rack of guns on the wall and grabbed a short-barreled M4 outfitted with a 100-round Beta C-mag, an Aimpoint red dot sight, and an attached Gemtech silencer on the muzzle.

"Luden, I'm getting my wife and coming back for my daughter. Then I'm getting the fuck out of here," Grayson said as he checked the chamber of the loaded rifle.

"Not so fast there, Mr. Ghost! That ain't all! At the risk of the data on the parasite existing on another Bio-Yomi campus, the New U.S. will be dropping a nuke on every Bio-Yomi site in the Territories. If you have even a slight awareness of the Bio-Yomi Territories, you'll know that you can't take a piss without sprinkling on a Bio-Yomi facility. If you were any good at math in school, then you'll remember the formula: the velocity of a rocket carrying a nuclear payload divided by it landing in every major city in the region simultaneously in six hours, equals you dying before you can save your wife and make it out of harm's way. If the blast doesn't get you, the radiation sure as fuck will," Rio informed Grayson as he tossed a gummy worm into the air and caught it in his mouth.

Luden finally rose from his chair and somberly approached Rio.

"I know you wouldn't let your family die out here. I *know* you wouldn't have come here if there wasn't a way out of this. Spill it," Luden demanded.

Rio rose from the couch, wiped his sticky hand on his slacks and coughed before straightening his cowboy hat and hiking up his belt.

"Well, cousin, you'd be right. There is a Bio-Yomi facility on the outskirts of Capital City. It's essentially a junkyard for defunct Bio-Yomi technology. In the basement, there is a weapon that will be able to… *POW!* Erase all of Hirohiko Naito's cells at the same time. You kill Naito before 6:00 a.m., we call off the nukes. And with the leader of the Territories dead, we scrub the Bio-Yomi systems by hand," Rio explained, offering them a speck of hope.

Luden, Kurt, and Grayson all glanced at each other, mentally preparing for a long night. Rio licked his fingers clean and held up his other hand.

"Now there's bad news, good news, and then news that will make you flip your shit. Bad news: you will need the one and only Sebastian Borka to help you... *prep*... the weapon, it being defunct and all. Good news: Sebastian Borka is in charge of that facility, being defunct himself, and is essentially Naito's prisoner there. Now, get ready to flip your shit: they are holding Faith in the same. Damn. Facility. Giggity, goddamn, I'm good! Let me hear a hallelujah for American intelligence!" Rio shouted as he danced in place.

Kurt placed his thumb to his chin and contemplated the situation as Luden rushed to his desk and began writing a note amongst the array of the firearms strewn about the tabletop.

"What exactly is the weapon we are looking for?" Grayson asked as he aggressively approached Rio, ready for action.

"I'm going to be honest; my source didn't tell me. Your guess is as good as mine," Rio replied, shrugging his shoulders.

"This is beyond fucked. You're coming with us, and if *anything* you said is a lie, I'll make sure you never lie again," Grayson barked, balling his prosthetic left hand into a fist.

"Woah there, Grayson! I am under strict, ball-squeezing orders to *not* get involved. Because, I am *not here*. If I so much as leave behind a fart cloud, my Government will 'disappear' me faster than you can say... gummy worm?" Rio responded defensively as he raised the bag of gummy worms, offering one to Grayson.

"Where do we find Naito after obtaining the weapon?" Grayson impatiently asked, his right hand squeezing the pistol grip of the M4.

"Where else? He'll be announcing his newfound... *ability*... on the rooftop of the main Bio-Yomi headquarters in Capital City. You know... the same rooftop you sent a bomb-ridden helicopter to in an attempt to assassinate him on Vax Day. Hopefully, this time... you'll get luckier," Rio cockily muttered to Grayson, winking at him.

Luden finished writing his note and advanced toward the group in the center of the room.

"Grayson, I'm scrambling the entire fighting force of the Psychophants to Bio-Yomi Tower. They'll be set to arrive at 5:00 a.m. sharp. It'll be tight, but it'll be an army. It's the best I can do. I don't want to step on your toes with Faith, so how do you want to handle the facility?" Luden asked, actually acting like a competent leader.

Grayson rested the M4 on his shoulder as his eyes darted back and forth, processing a plan.

"Luden, you and I leave for the facility right now. I go for the weapon, you go for Borka. If either one of us finds Faith along the way, we'll handle it. If not, we'll find her after. Then we haul ass to Bio-Yomi Tower where we'll vaporize Naito and end this shit. Kurt, you stay here. Prep the suit for Faith and help the Psychophants any way you can. I hope to god when we find her, we can get her to fight. Rio, you're fucking meeting us at Bio-Yomi Tower. I want you to see us snatch the life out of that fucker so you can call off the hounds the second it happens. Otherwise, you stay the *fuck* out of my way, Freedom Traitor," Grayson confidently ordered the group.

Grayson's cool confidence put Kurt's mind at ease, causing him to flash a jolly smile. Luden folded up the note of instructions for his men while Rio turned his empty bag of gummy worms upside down, shaking it.

As Grayson undid the lock bar on the steel door, he turned and paused for a moment.

"Luden, you make sure Emily stays in the bunker with the other kids… I…"

"Say no more," Luden quickly replied, interrupting Grayson's vulnerability.

Grayson flung open the door as they poured out of the room and went their separate ways.

Chapter 6

DEMON OF DEATH

A creaky wooden door flew open as Bryan, in his samurai armor, helped Faith walk through the doorway. As they entered, he flipped a switch on a small generator near the door, illuminating the room with dull, yellow light. Faith examined the only room of what amounted to a shack constructed of sheet metal with the flooring made out of crushed soda cans. A table crafted from twisted metal rested in the center of the room with an array of lab equipment sitting atop it. A bed seemingly crafted from half of a crushed car was perfectly slotted into the corner of the room, with a black footlocker featuring the red Bio-Yomi Torii gate logo sitting at the foot of the jury-rigged bed.

Bryan waved his arm and the odachi on his back floated toward the sheet-metal wall near the bed and magnetized to it.

"Here, I'm sure you need this…" Bryan mumbled sheepishly under his Tengu mask as a tin cup floated from the table into his hand.

Unsure of himself, he held the cup out to Faith.

"You said we would talk once we got here. Now we're here. I deserve answers… I thought…" Faith started, holding back the overwhelming emotions behind her words.

Bryan, with a shaky hand, removed the Tengu mask from his face, revealing silvery skin, blue lips, and a bald head. His eyes were cloudy and he tilted his face away from Faith in disgrace. He dropped the metal mask to the floor, walked over to the table, and set the cup down before placing his palms on the table's corners.

"Dad, what happened to you? You just *left*... Kurt said you got infected with the Vola virus and you didn't tell him where you were going. Just that you left the energy source with him..." Faith said as she kept her distance from him.

Bryan, with his weight on his arms pressing against the table, hung his head.

"Faith... I'm sorry... I think you could probably figure out that I didn't want you to see me like... Just... We all know what Vola did to people... When I left Bio-Yomi, I smuggled out two biomagnetic energy sources along with a case of Vax and all of the vaccine scientists' notes. I left one energy source with Kurt because he was partner to its creation and I took one with me.

"I drove across the desert to the same facility you were just now being held at. The symptoms started to hit me as I pulled into the parking lot. I rushed inside, popped open my briefcase, sprawled out the notes, and attempted to combine the biomagnetic energy source with the vaccine. I knew there were theories about combining them in order to heal your body, give you superhuman strength, etc. But as I was prepping the equipment, my body began to fail me. I fumbled the case of Vax and it landed on the energy source. There was a flash of light, and when I regained consciousness, I looked at my arms… They were just raw muscles and tendons. I looked down at my body, it was just cartilage and bone. There was no blood, no organs. And then my skin began to reform… But it was this dull silver…

"Faith, I'm not even sure if I can still be called your father. Right now, I'm just a walking corpse pulsing with electromagnetic energy. That's how I can… *move* certain things," Bryan explained, struggling to open up.

As he finished, he motioned around the room at the metal construction.

Faith took a shaky step toward him on her prosthetic leg. Then another.

"Dad, look at you… You're still *you*. Even I can see that. Except, you're finally a *samurai* now," Faith said, surprising herself with a short and airy giggle.

"I was planning on living out my dream and finally wearing this outfit if I learned I was going to die in that lab… God, it was so stupid. But it was just collecting dust in storage… I figured it would be a waste if I didn't put it on now," he admitted, laughing it off.

Faith approached the table and placed her hand over her father's, flinching a bit from the lack of warmth.

"Where have you been? Why didn't you come back to us?" she warmly questioned him.

Bryan glanced at Faith as he fought the knot in his throat.

"I wanted you to remember me the way I was *before*. And I didn't want Hirohiko to know I was still walking around. I wanted to find a way to shut down Bio-Yomi once and for all. Faith, I was vaccinated at Bio-Yomi. When I realized I was infected, I knew that he wanted me gone. He viewed me as a threat when I told him I was walking away from it all. That bastard didn't give me the vaccine; he gave me the Vola virus. And when I woke up from the mishap at the lab, with these... *powers*... I knew I could kill him and anyone else who would take over the company after him. But I was only one guy, I had to be smart about it. I was in Capital City, watching Hirohiko's every move when your incident in Red City happened. After that, I started watching over you and Emily at your bunker, as well. I'm sorry I wasn't there for you, Faith... I feel like I failed you..."

She squeezed his hand as her lower lip trembled.

"It's okay, Dad. I love you. And you're here now. I've got you back," she said lovingly as she rested her head on his shoulder.

Bryan stroked her hair, gently pushed himself away from her, and cleared his throat.

"Faith, I'm sorry. I wish we had more time... but we have work to do," Bryan stated, breaking the warm moment between them.

Faith stood up straight and quietly crossed her robotic arms over her stomach and nodded.

"How can I help you stop Naito? I saw what he's become..." she said, feeling helpless again.

"You aren't going to *help* me. We are going to kill that son of a bitch *together*," Bryan announced proudly as he walked toward the footlocker near the makeshift bed.

"Dad, I'm not the person you remember either... Look at me, I'm fucking useless. I'm not looking for pity, but I'm not ignorant either. These arms... These legs... I need to *feel* in order to fight. But with these... I can't feel anything..." Faith objected as she lifted her arms and turned her legs, disappointed in her own weakness.

Bryan knelt down, opened the footlocker and began to rummage through it.

"Faith, do you know why Kurt and I decided to make the biomagnetic energy source? Bio-Yomi was the world's leading company in prosthetics. When an incredible opportunity landed in front of us, we decided to turn that opportunity into something truly meaningful," Bryan reflected, pausing for a moment.

As he pushed aside a coat in the footlocker, a faint blue light washed across his face.

"Watching soldiers, victims of car accidents, workers who suffered factory mishaps, and people who were born without limbs... Watching the hope in their eyes when they saw our prosthetics... just... fade to tears as they realized the long road of rehabilitation required to live with those prosthetics... It broke our hearts. But, one after the other, they persevered and... with time... learned to get by. Their courage inspired us to make the biomagnetic energy source to boost their ability to adapt to their new limbs."

Bryan wrapped one hand around a small, glowing blue item and his other hand around a glossy, white sheath housing a katana. He deftly stood up and walked, with purpose, over to Faith. He laid the katana on the table and held out his fist that hid the glowing blue object.

"Sometimes in life, you just need a helping hand. I know for someone like you, it's hard to ask for help. Shame envelops you. You feel like you are a burden... and that you should be good enough to overcome it on your own. But the reality is... Even the strongest person runs out of steam and falls down. And if that person has lived a just and selfless life, someone *will* reach out a hand to help them back up. Faith, I'm not sure what more I can offer you, but this is *my* helping hand to you," he explained, unwrapping his fingers and revealing a fragment of a swirling electromagnetic energy source set in a platinum ring.

"This was your mother's ring. I'm... ready to let go of it now," he admitted, "In it, I set the fragment that was left after the explosion of my energy source. Go on, it's yours."

Faith hesitantly reached for the ring with her robotic left hand. She carefully pinched it between her fingers before bringing it close and inspecting it. It was a polished platinum wedding band with the words "Love you always" engraved on the inside of the band. Warmth washed over Faith's face as she could have sworn she saw her mother's reflection looking back at her from the polished surface of the ring.

"Go ahead, Faith," Bryan reassured her as he placed his gray hand on the sheathed sword on the table.

With apprehension, Faith eased the ring onto the ring finger of her right mechanical hand. The band sparkled in contrast to the black, carbon fiber of her finger.

As the ring came to rest at the base of her finger, the fragment of energy began to pulse. Faith watched as a warm, neon-blue energy wave flashed through her arm, causing the veins in her body to glimmer a bright blue for a moment. Her prosthetic legs began to lighten until she levitated an inch above the ground. Finally, her body temperature returned to normal and her veins ceased to glow as her feet reconnected with the ground. As she landed, her knees instinctively bent, taking up a fighting stance. A halo of energy shot out of her body blowing papers off of the nearby desk into the air.

Bryan, using his powers, launched the sheathed katana from the table toward Faith. Faith's left hand instinctively extended, catching the sheath, as her right hand reflexively unsheathed the sword. The blue glow from her ring glinted off of the polished blade as she studied the weapon. At the base of the blade, a single cherry blossom had been embossed in the shiny steel.

"After our last disagreement over my employment at Bio-Yomi, you gave me this sword that I had made for you and told me to throw it away. Well, I just now threw it away... Right back to you. Faith, tomorrow morning the New U.S. Government will be launching nuclear weapons all over the Bio-Yomi territories unless Hirohiko Naito is dead before 6:00 a.m. Your daughter, your husband, and the life that you've fought for will be *forfeit* if we don't kill him," Bryan solemnly informed her.

Faith tilted her head as she watched her wrist rotate three-hundred and sixty degrees, slowly manipulating her sword like a propellor. She stopped and stared at her reflection in the polished blade.

"And where can we find that old fucker?" She asked resolutely.

"He is scheduled to show off his godhood at six o'clock on top of Bio-Yomi Tower in Capital City. My Government contact should have met up with Grayson by now. They should be retrieving a weapon that can destroy Naito as we speak. But it will take all of us working together to even have a chance against him, his son, and his army. Faith," Bryan continued, "remember when I was training you for the World Kendo Championship, and we would spar every night?"

Faith rested the sword at her side and looked at him quizzically.

"Yeah," she responded, unsure of his implication.

"You asked if I ever went all-out with you… And I told you I didn't. Well, Cherry Blossom, let's spar one last time. I promise I will give you *everything* I have. Because *this time* we are training for the fight of our lives," Bryan told her as he raised his arms, causing the entire metal shack to instantly fragment and swirl around them.

He then slapped his hands together, turning it into a giant heap of scrap above them. Then he opened his fist, causing it to slam to the ground next to them. As dust rose from the heap, Bryan smiled and held his hand out toward the giant ball of scrap. His steel Tengu mask erupted from the pile and crashed into his hand as he caught it and placed it onto his face. His enormous odachi flipped into the sky from the pile and fell perfectly into his right hand.

"Do we have to yell with each strike for a point to count?" Faith jabbed as she tossed her sheath aside and held her katana at the ready.

"We've both fallen into fighting styles of dishonor to combat enemies who fight dirty. Fight as you would fight Hirohiko Naito! Give me everything you've got! Just like old times!" Bryan exclaimed with exhilaration under his mask.

Faith emitted a guttural war cry as she rushed toward her father, katana held high over her head. As she swiftly swung with a downward slice, he leaned to the side, cleanly dodging it. Faith's left foot shook a bit and collapsed, sending her falling to a knee. Bryan kicked her chest, sending her sliding backwards. She dug her hand and feet into the dirt and stood back up.

"Come on, Faith! Show me what *real* combat has taught you!" Bryan yelled at her.

This time, they charged at each other, and Bryan swung his 5-foot-long blade at a diagonal downward angle toward her shoulder. Faith smacked the side of the blade mid-swing with her robotic hand, sending it rocketing into the dirt. A thunderous boom shook the earth as a geyser of dust shot into the air.

Faith then performed a flexible spinning back kick, planting her metallic foot firmly into Bryan's chest. He slid through the dirt on his feet until he stopped himself with his off-hand.

"Come on, Dad! I thought you were supposed to be some kind of *samurai*!" Faith taunted with a grin across her face.

Bryan gently tossed his odachi in front of him as he closed his eyes, brought his fist with two fingers raised to his chest, and caught the sword with his magnetic ability. As the sword floated in front of him, he walked toward Faith, manipulating the sword to rapidly attack as he neared her.

The massive odachi relentlessly slashed at Faith from every angle as she dodged around the field and deflected its strikes with her own katana. When Bryan finally got within striking distance, he called his sword back to his hands and began thrusting and slashing with it. The heavy blade whipped through the air with immense force, causing Faith's hair to blow back with each attack. Faith dodged and deflected each slice as she put forth her own cunning counter attacks, causing Bryan to fumble and falter as he attempted to block them with his massive sword.

As Faith thrust her sword toward Bryan's temporarily exposed throat, he dropped his head down and blocked the attack with his mask. Sparks exploded from his face as he pushed his hand out toward Faith's sword, using a magnetic push to rip it from her hands and send it flying over her shoulder.

The sword *clanked* onto the ground and rolled through the dirt twenty-five yards away. Bryan horizontally slashed toward Faith's torso, but she bent over backwards, "limboing" under the attack. She fell onto her shoulder blades and somersaulted backwards, leaping from the ground and avoiding another slash from Bryan's blade.

She turned and ran toward her sword until she realized she did not hear pursuing footsteps behind her. She quickly turned around, her hair whipping from the inertia, and saw the odachi rocketing toward her like a spear.

Faith emitted a powerful yell as she slapped her hands together, catching the intimidating blade between her robotic hands. Bryan pulled his arm back, recalling the blade. As it began to slip through Faith's grasp, she closed her fingers around it and gripped it as tight as she could. She was lifted off the ground as she wrapped her legs around the sword, using the guard on the weapon's hilt as a place to leverage her feet.

As Faith neared Bryan on the flying odachi, she kicked the blade down, bouncing the pommel off of the ground. As the sword flexed, launched her forward, and flew straight into the sky, she planted a powerful kick onto Bryan's face. Sparks ignited off of Bryan's mask as Faith's robotic foot deeply scratched it during the flying kick. The mask was ripped from Bryan's head, revealing his silvery face as his eyes glistened like those of a father playing catch with his child.

He crashed backwards onto the ground as a puff of dirt rose from underneath him. After sliding to a stylish halt, Faith caught Bryan's falling odachi with a single hand held out at her side. The weight of the sword caused her wrist to tilt and the tip of the blade to pierce the earth beneath her. Faith wrapped her other hand around the lengthy handle as she ran toward Bryan with the tip dragging through the dirt.

With a final scream, the carbon fiber in Faith's arms flexed as the cords underneath glowed brightly with a teal hue. Engaging the synthetic and organic muscles in her body, she heaved the massive sword over her head. As she brought it crashing down onto Bryan, he reached out his hand and pressed an open palm toward the sword.

The odachi froze in mid-strike, just inches from his head. He let out a hearty laugh as he wiped a tear from his cheek with his other hand. Faith dropped the sword to the ground as her father stood up and gave her a bear hug.

"I love you so much, dad! Thank you…" Faith cried as he lifted her up.

"I love you, too, Cherry Blossom! You are *so* strong. And I'm so *proud*," Bryan told her as he lowered her back down and released her from his grasp.

Faith walked over to her sword, scooped it up from the ground, and placed it back into her sheath. Bryan placed his odachi onto his back and recalled his mask to his hand.

"Let's kill that fucker and end Bio-Yomi for good," Faith confidently declared to her father as she secured her sheathed sword to her waist.

"Once and for all," Bryan reiterated as they faced each other and respectfully bowed.

After completing their bow, they turned to look toward the dull glow of the distant Capital City across the desert. Bryan put his arm around Faith and pulled her close, squeezing her shoulder with determination as the dust from their duel settled around them.

CHAPTER 7
TACTICAL ESPIONAGE

L uden and Grayson sat in a blue, armored SUV across from the rundown Bio-Yomi facility. PSYCHOPHANTS was spray-painted in white along the body of the vehicle along with laughing skulls and bullets. The decrepit Bio-Yomi building sat one story tall, with a long, narrow layout. The lights in the facility were dead and the second letter "i" had fallen off of the Bio-Yomi sign out front.

"How many guys you figure are in there? Anthill or snake hole?" Luden asked as he racked a round with a *kachunk* into a Saiga-12 AK-shotgun with a comically large SilencerCo Salvo suppressor on the muzzle.

The lengthy silencer brushed the ceiling of the vehicle as he manipulated the firearm. The twelve-round box magazine protruded from the bottom of the gun and kept scraping the glove compartment in front of him.

Grayson sat in the driver's seat of the SUV and dodged the silencer as it whipped past his face.

"The fuck are you talking about? You ever wonder why I couldn't *stand* you back in the day? You say weird shit. *Anthill* or *snake hole*? Nukes are going to be raining down on us in a few hours and you're playing *This* or *That*?" Grayson vented as he retrieved his silenced M4 with the 100-round Beta C-mag from the backseat.

"Anthill would be a whole bunch of weak assholes. Snake hole would be just a few ultra-badasses. What do you think?" Luden clarified, ignoring Grayson's criticism.

Grayson slung the M4 across his chest in the tight quarters of the vehicle, then turned to look at Luden.

"Luden. It's *us*. It's going to be a fucking rabid hippopotamus parade in there. Just a hundred fucking unkillable death machines chasing us around like a fucking cartoon," Grayson snapped as he flailed his arms around, "Is that what you wanted to hear? Fuck it, I'm going."

The car door flung open with a swift kick from Grayson's boot. Luden opened his door, and struggled to remove his unwieldy automatic-shotgun from the vehicle. After some maneuvering, he exited and caught up to Grayson who was taking cover next to the entrance of the building.

Luden pressed his back against the wall as he caught his breath.

"Really? Front door? You said you were '*noodling*' on a plan in the car. What did you come up with?" Luden interrogated him in a hushed tone.

"We are going to walk in the front door. I go left, you go right. You find Borka, I find the weapon. We leave," Grayson flatly explained.

Luden scrunched his face and squinted his eyes.

"*What?*" Luden angrily whispered.

"We go in the front door—" Grayson began to say.

"No, no. I heard you the first time! We are just going to *wing it?*" Luden inquired genuinely.

Grayson shifted his weight to his other knee as he crouched near the wall of the building.

"We don't have a blueprint of the building, we don't have time to look around, and we are both a couple of gunslinging ass-kickers. Come on, we *live* for this shit. We just go stealthy for as long as we can," Grayson reassured him as he scratched his nose.

"Yeah, okay, fine. You're right. ThreeTwoOne, let's go!" Luden whisper-yelled as he pushed the front door of the building in and slipped through.

Grayson sighed as he caught the door and followed Luden through the entrance. The inside was barely illuminated by a weak emergency lighting system. Behind an abandoned reception desk was an unlit neon Torii gate symbol with a cracked Bio-Yomi sign underneath it. Next to the desk was a shadowy staircase leading downstairs with a dangling sign that read "Dangerous Materials." To the left was a hallway with a sign that read "Equipment Storage" and to the right was a hallway with a spot for a sign that was missing.

"I'm going to go left and check out equipment storage. The mystery hallway is all yours," Grayson whispered to Luden as they crouched in the lobby.

"Why don't you just go to the basement? I'll clear the first floor," Luden suggested, forgetting to whisper.

"Shhh, keep your voice down. We stick to the plan. I go left, you go right," Grayson reminded him.

"Oh, for fuck's sake. Some fucking plan——" Luden began to say, rolling his eyes.

Luden's heart froze as he saw a black, tactical helmet bobbing up the dark staircase from below. As the Bio-Yomi soldier's eyes reached their line of sight, his eyes widened and he gasped.

With an uncomfortably loud "PSSHHTT," Luden reflexively raised his suppressed shotgun and fired. A fist-sized pattern of 00 buckshot landed in the man's open mouth, tearing off his head above the jaw. The top of the soldier's head bounced down the stairs like a basketball, echoing with each impact of the helmet on the stairs. The pattering of bone fragments, teeth, and flesh impacting the walls and ceiling reverberated down the halls. A gurgling, airy, squeak eked from the man's neck as his tongue curled back, slid down his throat, and plugged his airway, before his body fell backwards and rolled down the stairs. His radio, rifle, and spare magazines clattered down the staircase along with his body until it came to rest at the bottom.

Grayson and Luden cringed and ducked their heads in anticipation as they listened for a few seconds after silence returned to the lobby. They looked around, looked at each other, and breathed simultaneous sighs of relief.

"So, I go right and you go left?" Luden confirmed as color returned to his face.

"Yep," Grayson simply replied.

Grayson made his way down the hallway and realized it came to an end fairly quickly with a sharp turn. As he rounded the corner, he stopped short and attempted to comprehend the amount of gore spread across the destroyed hallway.

A single emergency light flickered, illuminating the violent mess with intermittent flashes of dim light. Grayson could not determine how many men had been slaughtered in the hallway by the collection of limbs and fleshy chunks splattered across the walls, ceiling, and floor. A severed leg dangled from a hole in the ceiling, dripping blood onto a mutilated torso wearing a tactical vest that had been slashed clean through.

Taking a step forward, Grayson's boot squished into a thick puddle of blood that stretched to a set of double doors like a red carpet. Sloshing through the gore, Grayson passed a broken window in the hallway before reaching the doors at the end. With his prosthetic hand, Grayson eased the door open and stepped inside with his rifle held at a high-ready position.

As he slowly cleared the room, stepping over and around sliced-and-diced Bio-Yomi goons laying in a shallow river of their own fluids, he noticed a bloody handprint near the bottom of a heavily cracked wall at the back of the room. He approached the wall and held his own prosthetic hand up to the print. It matched the pattern his hand would have left; it was just a bit smaller.

"I don't know what the fuck did this, but something tells me I just missed you, Faith. Please be safe," Grayson mumbled to himself.

Grayson doubled back through the bloody stream in the hallway, rounded the corner to the lobby and carefully descended the stairs to the basement, passing the headless soldier and all of his equipment on the way down. He heard another "PPSSHHTT" echo through the lobby and down the stairs as he continued his descent into the basement.

A Bio-Yomi soldier that Luden had just blasted in the throat with buckshot, emitted the noise of a choking crow as his head dropped and dangled to the side of his body by a thin strip of meat. The soldier's boot slipped on the tile, causing his back to slam into the wall of the hallway before sliding down to the floor. Blood drained from the soldier's neck and head in abundant waves as his corpse sat up against the wall of the hallway.

Luden looked into the man's terrified eyes, whose head hung upside down next to his own shoulder. He felt the man's lifeless pupils peer deep into his soul.

"Don't look at me like that… If you weren't wearing all of that armor, I wouldn't have to shoot you guys there…" Luden awkwardly whispered to the deceased soldier.

The dead, blue eyes on the upside-down head continued to stare right through Luden.

"Ugghhhh," Luden groaned as a shiver ran down his spine and his shoulders convulsed.

Luden peeled his eyes away from the corpse and carefully continued down the hallway. But he couldn't shake the feeling that the dead body's eyes were following him.

"Goddamn heebie-jeebies…" Luden muttered, nearing a set of double doors at the end of the hallway.

As he approached the doors, he peeked through the small windows above the handles. Inside were ten Bio-Yomi soldiers rummaging through rows of cabinets and drawers in a laboratory that had been torn apart. Files, folders, shattered glass, and broken lab equipment littered the tables and floors of the room. At the back of the lab was a man wearing a white lab coat and sitting in a wheelchair with an open, manilla folder in his lap.

"*Anthill…*" Luden confirmed under his breath.

Luden took note of the soldiers' positions before backing away from the door, stretching his muscles, and rolling his shoulders.

"Okay, Luden. Time to flip the switch," he said, hyping himself up as he lightly slapped his cheeks.

He exhaled three quick breaths and ran at the doors, shoulder-charging through them. Firing his suppressed AK-shotgun while running, Luden transitioned from head to head on four unsuspecting soldiers who had been tossing files to the floor from a library-like row of shelves. A rhythmic *PSHT, PSHT, PSHT, PSHT* echoed through the room as the four soldiers' heads were liquified into red, pulpy messes, projecting wet viscera across the nearby shelves. As the bodies crashed to the ground and the runny, cranial remains splattered on the floor, Luden doubled back through the shelves, ran to the opposite side of the room, and took cover behind a laboratory cart.

"What the *fuck* was that?" a soldier across the room hollered.

"...fucking nail gun or something?" another soldier asked.

Luden, struggling to hide his obnoxiously long shotgun behind the cart, peeked out from cover and watched two soldiers approach the shelves with their rifles at the ready.

"They're fucking *dead*!" one of them yelled, causing the other soldiers in the room to scramble toward their location.

"Jesus... Fucking *shotgun shells*?" one of the new arrivals observed.

At that moment, the doors Luden had burst through finally slammed shut.

"Quick, out there!" one of the soldiers called out, pointing a gloved finger at the doors.

"You, and you, *on me*!" the first soldier ordered as a team of three Bio-Yomi soldiers rushed past the shelves and out the doors into the hallway.

Luden moved from cover and rounded the back of the room to flank them. His heart stopped and he paused for a moment as he locked eyes with the wheelchair-bound Sebastian Borka at the back of the room.

Borka, peering at Luden with his only remaining eye, held up one of his crooked fingers to his chapped lips. Luden nodded and continued sneaking up behind the soldiers.

"Fuck… Wanna draw straws to see who tells Pete's wife? Poor fuck asked to transfer here after she got knocked up. This wasn't supposed to happen…" one of the soldiers lamented with a heavy tone.

"*Pete*? What about Bradley and Ramirez? Or Chang?" a second soldier responded.

"Eh, fuck those guys. They were scumbags. Well, Chang was all right. Kinda quiet, though," the first soldier answered as he nudged one of the headless corpses with his boot.

The third soldier slapped the second one's helmet.

"Radio down to Sasaki in the basement, tell him we've got a turd in the pie," the third soldier ordered.

The second soldier reached toward the radio on his vest as a thick spray of warm liquid splashed onto his face and into his eyes. Through squinting eyelids, he watched as his headless comrade fell to the ground with blood pulsing from his neck onto the tile. His other compatriot turned to run toward the double doors as a loud *PSHT* cracked behind him and a string of buckshot connected with the back of his neck. His head popped off of his torso like a cork as his body continued to run ahead.

As his headless body crashed into the wall, a thick splash of blood erupted from his neck as if from a sloshing paint can, before falling to the ground and twitching.

Hands shaking, the surviving soldier slowly turned around, blinking his blood-speckled eyes, as he came face-to-face with the large, smoking bore of Luden's twelve-gauge silencer. Luden peeked over the sights of the shotgun and smirked.

"Wanna live?" Luden rhetorically asked as the soldier timidly nodded.

The three soldiers who had left the room doubled back down the hallway toward the double-doors to the lab. As they kicked the door in, they were greeted by the blood-drenched surviving soldier.

"We didn't see anyone… The fuck is going on here?" the lead soldier desperately asked.

The surviving soldier pointed to his left. The three soldiers all looked where he pointed as Luden, who was hugging the wall next to the doors, shot all three of them in the napes of their necks. Three torrents of blood, skin, and esophageal tissue completely covered the surviving soldier, further drenching him as if he were in the splash zone of a slaughter house.

Luden revealed himself to the soldier from the shadows as he rested his shotgun across the back of his shoulders.

"If I let you go, are you going to come back and kill me?" Luden asked the soldier who was trembling and dripping with a nigh-unfathomable amount of warm, coppery blood.

"N-n-n-n-no," he shakily replied, accidentally tasting a mixture of the other soldiers' blood as he opened his mouth.

Luden lowered his shotgun to hip level and fired with one hand, emitting a final loud *PSHT*. The top half of the soldier's head popped like a pressurized zit as his body fell over backwards, stiff as a board.

A smoking, spent shotgun shell ejected from the action of Luden's firearm and the impact of the hollow, plastic casing on the floor resounded through the still room. Luden pressed the magazine-release lever with his thumb and rocked the empty magazine out of the gun. He exchanged it for another fully loaded magazine from his back pocket, rocked it into the Saiga-12's magwell, and charged the bolt handle, loading a new green shell into the chamber.

"Impressive… You must be Mr. Luden," Borka weakly shouted from the back of the room.

Luden stepped over the last soldier's body as he shuffled in between two tables in the center of the room to reach Borka.

"Are you here for the same reason we are?" Borka asked as Luden dragged over a stool from a nearby table.

Luden took a seat, rested his shotgun across his lap, and wiped a few dots of blood from his face with his black sleeve.

"Well, I doubt it. Unless you are here to pick up a weapon than can one-shot your newly invulnerable corporate overlord," Luden responded, running his hand through his hair.

"A *weapon* to destroy Mr. Naito? We were sent here to find *old notes* that might be able to detail *how* to kill Mr. Naito.

The source of his power was once destroyed by the researchers who discovered it. Mr. Naito and his son tasked me with discovering how they did it so we could protect him from having a potential weakness exploited. I salvaged the source itself, you see… but no information exists on how the researchers disposed of the original," Borka feebly explained through a row of mostly missing teeth.

Luden tapped his trigger finger against the receiver of his shotgun as he listened to the explanation.

"Yeah, yeah, I heard the story from someone else. Fact is, we know how to kill Naito. And *you* are going to help us do it. You created this fucking monster, we need your help to un-create him," Luden hurriedly ordered him.

Borka's lips began to quiver as he looked down at his missing legs, ran his tongue through the gaps in his teeth, and tried to cry from an eye that no longer existed.

"I.. *cannot*… if we fail… they will…" Borka began to stammer.

Luden stood up from his stool, walked over to a nearby counter and leaned against it. He reached into a cargo pocket on his black, tactical pants and removed what appeared to be an ornate cigarette case. He opened it and removed a small, silver syringe filled with blue liquid. He rolled up the sleeve of his tactical turtle neck and injected the Vax into the clammy crease below his bicep. He rolled his eyes back and released a sigh before placing the empty syringe back into the case and pocketing it.

Luden collected himself and rolled his sleeve back down.

"You're not the only one that's been fucked by Bio-Yomi. They preached supporting freedom and opposing the bureaucratic red tape of the Government... then they turned around and got nearly the entire world addicted to a vaccine over a secret agenda. Then, they *profited* off of the damn addiction. When we decided to split from the Government and stay here under Bio-Yomi's rule, we just replaced one backstabbing set of masters for another. Fuck us, right?" Luden preached as he crossed his arms.

He pushed himself away from the counter and began pacing in front of Borka's chair.

"Apparently the almighty New U.S. Government draws the line at an invulnerable super human with the entire world in his back pocket. If we *fail*, they'll be nuking every one of your facilities in the Bio-Yomi Territories. 6:00 a.m. on the dot. Now, Faith told me that you are a surprisingly *caring* man. I don't know about you, but I'd be willing to risk getting tortured again if it meant a chance at saving the lives of innocent people in the Territories. You saved three people when you gave Faith the Izanami suit. Now, how about you save millions more?" Luden implored, stopping in front of Borka and looking into his eye.

Borka's eye closed for a moment as he breathed deeply through his nose. He opened his eye and held up his disfigured hand before balling it into a fist.

"How can I help kill Hirohiko Naito?" Borka asked, steeling himself.

Luden crouched down to Borka's level and rested the buttstock of his shotgun on the ground.

"Naito can be killed if every single cell in his body, down to the last molecule and atom, is destroyed simultaneously. Apparently, there is a weapon in the basement that can do this, but we were told that we'll need your help to prep it," Luden explained, catching him up to speed.

Borka cracked half of a smile as he clasped his deformed hands across his lap.

"*Prep* it... Very amusing... There is no guarantee that a nuclear blast will be able to destroy every cell simultaneously in Mr. Naito's body. It is a *probably* at best, but most likely a *maybe*. The Government must know this. This is the true reason they intend to bomb all Bio-Yomi facilities... If they can cripple his influence, perhaps they can gain allies if their attack fails. There *is indeed* a weapon in this facility capable of destroying Mr. Naito all at once. But, 'prepping it' is a bit of an understatement. We must get started at once. If you wouldn't mind..." Borka mentioned as he motioned towards the handles of his wheelchair.

Luden slung his shotgun across his back, grabbed ahold of Borka's wheelchair, and made his way toward the exit of the room.

Chapter 8

FULL CIRCLE

Grayson removed a bright, handheld flashlight from his back pocket and shined it into the vast, pitch-black basement. The sizable room was a dank graveyard of discarded prosthetic limbs. All generations of Bio-Yomi appendages along with their dented and cracked cases littered the floor and filled shelves that lined the walls.

As he shuffled through the limbs like a ball-pit, his flashlight picked up a glint from a pile in the middle of the room. He approached it and saw a long, bloody, steel screw poking out of a pile of limbs. Grabbing the screw, he lifted it out of the pile, and realized that it was attached to a prosthetic leg. The leg began to whir and rotate as if it were trying to screw into something. Spooked by the sudden sound and movement, Grayson tossed it aside into another pile and shined his light around the room.

At the back of the basement, against a wall, was a workbench with an enormous, carbon fiber case sitting atop it. Grayson waded through piles of junk until he reached the table and gazed upon the case.

He brushed off a layer of dust with his hand and shined his flashlight on the lid.

It read:

Project SF: Left

Property of Bio-Yomi

Authorization: K.N.

Underneath the text was a red Torii gate that sparkled under the bright beam of the flashlight. Grayson popped the catches around the case, breaking the airtight seal, and cautiously lifted the lid.

A dull, blue glow emanated from the case and illuminated its contents as Grayson released the hinged lid. Inside, he gazed upon a gargantuan steel left arm, identical to Steel Fist's right arm. Grayson removed a handwritten letter from the case and read it to himself with the help of his flashlight.

Steel Fist has exceeded an output of 120% in his current configuration.

I'm afraid adding an additional "Fist" could result in a detonation

of the last complete biomagnetic energy source we have left.

Since reverse engineering the source is too dangerous,

it is impossible to increase output to safe levels

despite the reduced size of this prototype.

I am requesting it be decommissioned.

-Head of Bio-Yomi R&D

Sebastion Borka

Grayson raised his prosthetic hand, held it between himself and the steel fist, and turned it back to front, inspecting it.

"If anything can vaporize a human down to his last hair, it's this damn thing. We might *actually* have a shot at this," he mumbled to himself as he closed the lid on the case and sealed it shut.

He pocketed his flashlight, heaved the case onto the ground and extended a carry handle, enabling him to pull it like a suitcase. As he took a step forward, he noticed a small flame burning in a shadowy corner of the basement. Coming from the direction of the tiny fire, a muffled cough echoed through the darkness.

"Someone else down here?" asked a raspy voice that sounded like it was talking into a bucket.

Grayson slowly placed his right hand on the pistol grip of the M4 slung across his chest and pointed it from his hip toward the flame, flicking the safety off with his thumb. He grasped the handle of the fist's case with his prosthetic hand and slowly took another step forward into the underground landfill of broken parts.

"*I heard that…*" the raspy voice taunted.

A forty-foot-long wall of fire erupted from the tiny flame, roasting the table Grayson had just left. The crackling fire lit up the basement, exposing Grayson and illuminating the source of the fire.

In the corner of the room stood Brazier, stitched head-to-toe in charred body armor, clutching his chest just right of his sternum. He removed his firefighter's mask and dropped it to the floor as he stared down Grayson. Brazier coughed a few times as blood dribbled down his heavily burned face. His hair, eyebrows, and ears had completely melted away.

"Quite the treasure trove, wouldn't ya say? I woke up down here all fucked up… and decided to help myself," he cheekily commented as he held up a hand-sized, metallic triangular prism with a tiny, blue orb in the center.

He slammed the prism into his chest, and layers of flexible, metal scales shot out from the object and encased his entire body in a skin-tight metallic shell. The glowing fire at the back of the basement reflected off of his shiny, full suit of midnight-black scaled armor.

"Now *that's* what I'm fuckin' talkin' about! Say… watcha got *there*?" Brazier pried, as his completely covered face turned toward the case that Grayson was pulling.

Grayson feigned lowering his weapon for a moment before snapping it back up and releasing a full-automatic volley of armor-piercing 5.56mm rounds toward Brazier. The bullets all slipped right off of the slick, black armor and pierced the wall behind him.

"If ya aren't gonna tell me… I guess I'll hafta have a look for myself," Brazier shouted under the full-body metallic suit as he aimed his flamethrower at Grayson.

With all of his might, Grayson pulled at the heavy case as he desperately kicked through the piles of prosthetic limbs. The heat of the flames cooked the back of his neck as he heard heavy footfalls methodically pursuing him.

As Grayson made it to the base of the stairs, he turned to look behind him and saw that the entire basement had been set ablaze. From the heart of the flames emerged

Brazier, who was laughing maniacally under the suit with his flamethrower pointed straight up, painting the ceiling with fire.

Brazier lowered his weapon once more and unleashed another fiery blast toward Grayson. Barely rounding the corner in time to escape the blaze, he dragged the case over the dead soldier at the bottom of the stairs and scrambled up the steps.

Grayson crawled up the stairs backwards as he used both hands to pull the case up, step-by-step.

Only ten steps away from the top, Brazier rounded the corner at the bottom of the stairs and stomped on the dead soldier's fiery body. His foot punched clean through the corpse's crispy ribcage as he raised his flamethrower and pointed it upstairs.

Grayson jerked the case with a mighty tug and dove around the corner and into the lobby as a wall of fire shot past him. As he made his way back to his feet, he encountered Luden pushing Borka in his wheelchair.

"The fuck was that?" Luden asked, surprised by the fiery explosion.

"Snake-hole…" Grayson managed to say in between coughs.

Brazier made it to the top of the stairs with his entire black, metallic suit rippling with dancing flames.

"*Luden*! What a happy fuckin' surprise! Looks like it's not too late to cash in on torchin' your ass, after all…"

As he leveled his flamethrower toward Luden, Grayson, and Borka, the pilot light flickered a few times before shrinking back into its thin, metal tube. He squeezed the trigger and nothing but a pathetic fizzle emerged from the weapon.

"*God* fucking *dammit*, can I get a god-damned *break* tonight?" Brazier shouted from underneath his armor as he pitched his flamethrower past the group and out a window into the parking lot.

Brazier pounded a scaley, metallic fist into his palm with a *clank*.

"Old man Naito's gonna pay me *big* when I bring in pieces of all three of ya!"

Seizing the opportunity, Luden ran backwards through the exit of the building, kicking it open and pushing Borka in his chair. Grayson grabbed the large case and promptly followed him. As they both ran toward their vehicle in the parking lot, Borka reached back and grabbed Luden's arm.

"That is the Onyx-Scale Armor. If one of his armored hands touches the prism on his chest, the armor will retract," Borka shakily informed Luden as he vibrated over the asphalt in his chair.

The brick wall next to the entrance of the building collapsed as Brazier effortlessly and causally walked through it in pursuit of the group, cracking the asphalt outside with each step. He staggered a bit as he coughed blood into the suit, but he managed to collect himself and push forward.

As the group arrived at the vehicle, Grayson and Luden tossed their long-guns into the backseat. Luden lifted Borka and slid him into the passenger seat of the vehicle while Grayson tossed his wheelchair into the trunk. Grayson left the heavy case near the tail lights and approached Luden, who was slamming closed the back door of the armored SUV.

"Run or fight?" Grayson asked in a hurry as he watched Brazier pick up the pace of his footsteps.

"This guy isn't going to give up. Borka said one of his hands has to touch his chest to drop the armor," Luden quickly explained to Grayson.

Luden reached into the small of his back and pulled out his snub-nosed .500 Smith and Wesson magnum revolver and placed it into Grayson's hand.

"This should have enough punch to move his hand. He'll be coming after me, so get the angle and make the shot. My life's in your hands, Grayson. Don't fuck it up," Luden commanded as he ran toward the approaching Brazier.

Grayson broke off from Luden and ran into the bushes surrounding the building to flank Brazier.

Luden stopped in the middle of the parking lot immediately in front of Brazier who was now facing him down.

"Well, *Luden*. This time—" Brazier began to wheeze.

Pop! Pop!

Luden had unholstered his 9mm Staccato 2011 and fired two shots at Brazier's chest. The bullets skipped off of the armor and ricocheted into the night. One went through a window of the smoking building and the other hit the asphalt behind him, sending chunks flying.

"Can I just finish a *fucking* sentence?" Brazier begged with rage building in his voice.

"From what your wife told me, you can't finish much of anything," Luden quickly jabbed.

"That's it, you mother fucker. I'm gonna paint the parking lot with your guts!" Brazier screamed as he rushed toward Luden.

Luden dodged three strikes as Brazier sloppily threw wide-swinging punches. A haymaker rocketed over Luden's head as he ducked under it and rolled between Brazier's legs. Brazier turned around and continued to unleash a flurry of punches that Luden fought to keep up with. Brazier then lifted his leg and hurled a roundhouse kick toward Luden's chest. Luden raised his forearms and blocked the blow, but it knocked his arms away and slammed him down onto his knees.

Brazier raised his arms straight out to his sides, preparing to smash Luden's head in between his hands.

BOOM!

...

Ting!

Grayson, found an angle for his shot and touched off a round from the .50 caliber revolver. The five-hundred grain, hardcast lead bullet connected with the back of Brazier's hand, causing it to launch forward like a hinged gate and smack himself in the chest. The glossy black scales retracted from Brazier's body back into the prism on his chest.

On his back, Luden fired two rounds from his Staccato into Brazier's collar bones, shattering them before Brazier could reach for his chest again.

Luden then fired two rounds into Brazier's knee caps, leaving ragged exit wounds in the backs of his knees. Brazier collapsed to the ground and his melted face began to contort with pain as drips of blood formed a puddle underneath him.

"Why… why can't I… *kill… you?*" Brazier gasped and wheezed.

"I don't know, man. Because you're a fucking loser? What answer are you looking for here?" Luden asked as he sat up.

"*Am…* I? Heh… Heh… White… Phosphorous…" Brazier began to laugh as he removed an incendiary grenade from his belt and slipped his thumb through the pin.

BOOM!

Brazier's facial skin violently twisted and tore off of his head as the back of his skull and all of its contents were ejected through his mouth. His entire head liquified into a crimson jelly that splattered onto the cracked asphalt.

Luden shielded his face with his arm as pink mist rained down on him. He then stared at Braziers body as it fell to the side, revealing Grayson twirling the .500 magnum on his finger.

"Now *this… This* is a fucking revolver! I've got to say… I'm jealous, Luden!" Grayson shouted as Luden stood up from the ground, ripped the triangular prism from Brazier's chest, and walked toward him.

"Keep it. Ammo for that is impossible to find and it only has two shots left. It's more *your* style anyway," Luden offered as he rested his hands on his knees, catching his breath before continuing toward Grayson.

"Thanks, Luden," Grayson replied as they made their way back toward their vehicle, "You know, I just saved your ass."

"Yeah, well I saved yours first. And I saved it once before that," Luden reminded him.

"That was *after* you abandoned me on that mission! I had to run—" Grayson started to complain as he opened the driver's side door of the armored SUV and got in.

"Yeah, yeah, you ran ten city blocks with no ammo… I was *infected*, Grayson," Luden said as he got into the back seat and they closed the doors behind them.

Chapter 9
PIT STOP

The suspension on the blue, armored SUV flexed as Grayson hopped over a curb and brought the vehicle to an abrupt halt in front of a two-lane, blacktop road. A sign on the side of the road had a hand drawn yellow arrow pointing left that read: "Capital City," another sloppy black arrow pointing right that read: "Excelsior," and a red, right-pointing arrow labeled: "Red City."

"So, let's talk about the elephant in the car… what's it going to take to put that abomination of an arm on me?" Grayson asked, staring straight ahead and flexing his own bionic arm.

"It will be fairly straightforward since you already have a Bio-Yomi arm. But I will still need access to proprietary Bio-Yomi equipment to attach it. Unless you have that lying around… We are dead in the water…" Borka faintly answered, attempting to recover from the stress of their previous encounter.

Luden leaned forward from the backseat and popped his head out from between the two front seats. He glanced left and right, addressing both of them.

"Remember how I won my bid for leader of the Psychophants after ransacking what was left of the Bio-Yomi R&D headquarters? Well… everything in the lower levels was pretty much untouched by the explosion. We have *all* of that gear back at Excelsior."

Grayson glanced at his rugged G-shock watch. The hands pointed to 4:30 a.m.

"Fuck, we don't have much time. How long will it take, Borka?"

"You are missing your left arm up to your shoulder, yes?" Borka asked.

"Mmm-hmm," Grayson nodded, as Borka responded with a soft chuckle.

"The luck that follows your family is truly intriguing. Since compatible wiring is already in place, it should not take more than ten-minutes to install. It would only take five-minutes if…" Borka paused as he woefully held up his incomplete hands.

"I'm not sure I'm *that* lucky… It's an hour drive back to Excelsior, then it'll be a ninety-minute drive from there to Capital City. Luden, we're just going to have to go fight Naito without the fist. Borka, is there any way you could rig this thing to blow?" Grayson grasped at straws, desperate for an answer.

Borka just gently shook his head side-to-side.

"The device does not inherently have enough power on its own to completely destroy Mr. Naito upon detonation. In fact, there is a complication in powering the fist that I need to discuss with you privately… Yes, I could find a way to transform the device into an explosive, but I'm afraid I do not have the time to engineer something like that… We would all be shadows on the ground before I could complete it... I am sorry, Grayson," Borka confessed with empathy.

Luden suddenly smacked the back of Grayson's headrest.

"Don't discount that luck of yours just yet!" Luden shouted as he kicked open the back door of the SUV and ran out into the middle of the road, waving his arms.

A wall of dirt blew with the wind into the desert as the caravan of Psychophant warriors roared down the dusty road in the distance.

"I'll be damned," Grayson muttered as he exited the vehicle and leaned against the thick, armored hood.

The lead vehicle in the caravan was a semi-truck outfitted with welded-on steel plates and long, sharp spikes. It was painted maroon red with flaming skulls and "PSYCHOPHANTS" stylistically painted all over it. As it came to a stop in front of Luden, the rest of the caravan followed suit and slowed to a halt. The Psychophants all yipped and yelled, hyping themselves up for battle, as they battered the sides of their vehicles through open windows.

Slice, the thin Psychophant with a soul patch on his chin, hopped out of the passenger side of the semi-truck and approached Luden.

"Hey there, Boss! We're right on time and we are going to shove this whole damn army right up Bio-Yomi's ass!" he confidently yelled as he moved his dirty goggles to his forehead and lowered the bandana from his face.

"I knew I could count on you, Slice. You never fail to impress. But, I don't see that Government man with you… he still hanging around Excelsior?"

Slice brushed the dirt off of his nose as a grin took over his face.

"It's real funny you should mention that, Boss. He asked where our Bio-Yomi goods were and started settin' up a bunch of equipment. Said he was expectin' Mr. Grayson to come back with that 'Yomi scientist. His chopper was landin' right about the time we left."

"That son of a bitch, he had this all planned out…" Luden said under his breath.

Luden turned to look at Grayson who had already hopped back into the SUV and was pulling onto the road.

"Hold them off 'till I get back! I just have a quick pit-stop to make!" Grayson yelled through the open window as he pulled up next to Luden.

"Will do, Grayson. And say hi to my cousin for me, I knew that shifty bastard was up to something…" Luden acknowledged, smacking the side of Grayson's vehicle with the side of his fist.

"I have no idea where you people find each other," Borka mused from the passenger seat as he observed the seemingly endless line of vehicles retrofitted for war.

Grayson slammed his foot into the accelerator and watched the speedometer climb. He drove past nearly one-hundred Psychophants vehicles, all cheering him on, as he raced toward Excelsior. Halfway through the convoy, Kurt sat in his van, and upon seeing Grayson rapidly approaching, reached out the window and offered a friendly wave. Grayson made eye contact with Kurt and nodded at him as he whizzed by.

"And the knight moves across the board," Kurt muttered to himself, "God, I hope this works."

An hour later, at 5:30 a.m., Grayson drifted onto a dirt road as rocks pelted the undercarriage of his SUV. A *low fuel* warning flashed behind the steering wheel on the dash as he neared the gates to Excelsior.

Borka braced one of his hands against the dash in front of him as the gates to Excelsior parted. Grayson blew through them as they were halfway open, scraping the sides of the vehicle and ripping off the side mirrors.

Groups of children, elderly men, and women all lined up, making a pseudo-path through the ragged city. The SUV began to lurch and the engine sputtered as children ran alongside the car pointing to a steel-reinforced building that used to be an old gas station. The New U.S. Government helicopter sat next to the structure as the pilot inside played a video game on a portable device.

The vehicle ran out of fuel one-foot shy of a rusted gas pump as Grayson exploded out of the car. Three women in tan, greasy overalls opened the passenger door, lifted Borka out of the car and placed him into the wheelchair that a couple of teenage boys had retrieved from the back of the SUV.

Grayson grabbed the handles of Borka's wheelchair and hurriedly pushed him into the doorway of the gas station. One of the teenage boys retrieved the heavy case with Steel Fist's spare arm in it and followed them, struggling to catch up.

As they entered the gas station, the room was completely cleared out and a complex operating chair sat in the middle of the floor. Cables weaved between Bio-Yomi labeled carts loaded with tools and plugged into several running generators.

Rio snapped a blue latex glove over his right hand as he cracked a shit-eating grin.

"Ah, Grayson! I wasn't expecting you, but please, make yourself at home!" he announced sarcastically, still wearing his crocodile-skin cowboy hat.

Grayson, ignoring him, rushed toward the operating chair as Borka wheeled himself to one of the tables, retrieved several drill-like devices, and laid them in his lap. The teenage boy finally caught up with the case in tow and handed it off to Rio who rolled it over to the chair. A vibrant blue light washed across his face as he kicked the lid open.

"I'll be damned like a demon! Who woulda thought they built another fist for that fucker. Shit, I didn't realize it was this big! Looked smaller in the video!" Rio said cockily, winking at Grayson.

Borka wheeled himself over to the operating chair as Grayson leaned back and laid his prosthetic arm on a metal, off-shooting table. Pushing the drill-like device into Grayson's shoulder, Borka began to remove panels from Grayson's arm.

"You know, that video of you fighting Steel Fist made its rounds. Most governments tried to build a Steel Fist of their own, but without the damn energy source, they couldn't do it. You know, you almost had the fucker Grayson. It was an unfair fight and you *almost fuckin' had him*. You did better than any man that I know could've done," Rio said as he leaned over Borka's shoulder, popping jelly beans into his mouth from a small package.

The drill slipped from Borka's three-fingered hand and slammed onto the floor. Rio picked it up and handed it back to Borka, who diligently continued his work.

"So, you knew how this was all going to play out, huh?" Grayson asked Rio as Borka began to drill into a panel in Grayson's armpit.

Rio popped another jelly bean into his mouth as he annoyingly nodded his entire body.

"Well, I didn't *know*... But I was pretty sure you'd be able to pull it off. Luden's letter instructed the Psychophants to prepare for battle and for Excelsior to follow my lead. But, you know, I didn't know it would be a fuckin' *Steel Fist arm*, I'll tell you that.

My contact claimed to be a former Bio-Yomi scientist. Reached out from an unlisted computer at that defunct site you were at and informed the Government what was going on and how to win. Of course, the Government laughed at the message and just said, 'Launch the nukes!' Well, I still got family over here. So does my pilot. We snuck across the airspace... and here we are. Putting all of our eggs in your basket," Rio elaborated, fishing a piece of jelly bean from his molars with his tongue.

Borka began to shimmy Grayson's arm back and forth as Grayson winced and looked up at Rio.

"When we were in that facility… Faith was gone, but not by long. There had to have been twenty dead Bio-Yomi soldiers left behind. Completely shredded to bits. Any idea what happened there?" Grayson asked as he grimaced from Borka pulling on his arm.

"Yeah, not a fuckin' clue on that one, chief," Rio responded as he dumped three more jelly beans into his mouth.

Grayson's prosthetic arm broke loose and Borka tossed it to the ground with a heavy *thunk*.

"*You*… Place the arm onto the table," Borka ordered Rio as he motioned toward the off-shooting table on the operating chair.

Rio reached into the case, wrapped his hands underneath the arm, and lifted with his legs. He slowly eased the weaponized arm onto the table as Borka pushed up his glasses.

"Grayson… This arm was designed to work with a full-sized biomagnetic energy source. Faith's father, Bryan, was able to manufacture only two sources in his entire career at Bio-Yomi. One, he broke into fragments to potentially power multiple devices. He stole two of these fragments when he left the company. One more went missing; it was suspected that Kurt stole one, as well.

The other full-sized source was later used to power Steel Fist under Kimberly Naito's orders. The full-sized source in Steel Fist along with the conductivity of the Vax in his system is what allowed him to infinitely use the fist to its full potential. This lone fist has but a small fragment in it. By itself, it will not have enough energy to destroy Mr. Naito. But if we inject Vax into your body to act as a conductor… you will be able to perform one fully-powered attack. Then the fragment will shatter and it will most likely… *take your life* when it does… I know it will not change your mind since we are out of time and options… but I thought you should know before I attach it to your body," Borka informed Grayson.

Grayson saw a flash of his brother, Carlton's, face flash through his mind followed by the warmth of holding Emily's little hand.

"Fuck it. Strap it on, doc," Grayson said through a cold exterior.

Borka exhaled and began to maneuver the shoulder of the arm toward Grayson's torso.

Rio awkwardly looked around for a moment before walking in front of the operating chair and facing Grayson.

"Um… if this shit goes south… the radiation is going to decimate this shitty little place. I know if *my* daughter were here… I'd want her with me. Should I…" Rio spoke, for the first-time lacking confidence.

Grayson looked at Rio through his eyebrows and gave him a single nod. Rio showed Grayson a smile of understanding and exited the building.

Borka switched to a different tool in his lap and finished securing the second arm intended for Steel Fist onto Grayson's body. Grayson felt a strange buzzing in the arm as the electromagnetic energy fragment swirled in the bicep.

He opened and closed the thick, steel fingers, heavily clanging them against his palm. He then lifted the arm off the table and moved it around as he inspected the various vents, cables, and crevices on the weapon that once terrorized him and Faith.

Borka wheeled over to a nearby table that had a Vax case with the Bio-Yomi symbol on it, opened it, and retrieved a metal syringe filled with blue liquid.

"Considering we have less than twenty-minutes until this ends one way or another, we won't have to worry about this dose running out… Would you like *me* to do it, or…" Borka awkwardly suggested as he wheeled up to Grayson, holding out the syringe.

Grayon's consciousness was swept away into his grungy apartment the day before Vax Day. He sat at the round, kitchen table in the cramped, dank space with his brother Carlton. Carlton's skinny frame rocked back in his chair as his weaselly face fell blank.

"You know Grayson… When you *serve*, you think you are ready to die for your country… for *freedom*. As you grow up, movies, video games, television shows… they all show the impact you can make. The *difference* you can make. The inspiration of heroism and how it can influence those who come after you. I'm tellin' ya. When you have a fuckin' kid… It *all* goes out the window. At least it did for me. Kids go from being these obnoxious fucking creatures to literally your entire life. *They* become your reason. For *anything* you do. Good or bad. I'm tellin' ya… Being a parent, it's a beautiful thing. But in our profession… It's a fuckin' weakness," Carlton rationalized as he spun a silver ring on his left ring finger.

"Carlton, I'm sorry about Jessica and Luke… I mean, there's a reason we're fighting *against* the Government. We *saw* what they became. The things we had to do overseas… Not for *America*… But for the disgusting elites that run the show. They didn't care about collateral damage overseas… So why in the fuck would they care about collateral damage when they turned on us here at home? It was only a matter of time…" Grayson said gently.

Carlton slammed the legs of his chair onto the floor and ran his fingers through his thin, greasy hair.

"Yeah, well… It don't matter anymore, anyway. They're just another fuckin' casualty of war. Grayson, just like I promised mom and dad when we were kids… I'm gonna look out for you. But you're the only fuckin' person on the planet I'd die for, anymore. I'm just glad you and Faith can't even *have* kids. 'Cause when you hold that little shit in your hands on the day it's born, you just feel in your gut that you'd *kill*… and you'd *die* to save it. No matter what. I pity any man that has to feel weakness like that," Carlton bitterly said as he stood up from his chair and walked out of the room to hide his tears.

Grayson stared ahead silently, arms crossed as he contemplated whether or not to tell his brother that Faith was pregnant.

"…would you prefer to do it?" Borka finished asking as he held out the vaccine.

Grayson looked around the room, realized he was back in the operating chair, and stared at the syringe for a moment.

"Just get it over with," Grayson shortly replied.

Borka released a sigh of understanding, pressed the needle into Grayson's human arm, and depressed the plunger.

The electromagnetic fragment in Grayson's steel arm flashed, then began to pulse and swirl faster. The flexible metal covering his bicep flexed and inflated as Grayson felt a surge of power course through his veins.

"When you see your chance, close your fingers one at a time, pinky-to-thumb and pull your arm back as if to punch. This will initiate the charging process for the full-powered detonation. Other than that, I'm afraid that I've done all I can do to help you. The fight is yours now," Borka softly explained, placing his disfigured hand on Grayson's shoulder.

Grayson stood from the chair, rolled the shoulder of his new, massive arm a few times, and proceeded toward the exit.

"And Grayson," Borka shouted, "Faith was at the facility. If you did not find her there, it is likely she escaped."

"If I know Faith," Grayson replied, turning his head toward Borka, "she's already at Bio-Yomi Tower bodying those mother fuckers."

Borka smirked with approval at the thought of Faith tearing down Bio-Yomi once more as Grayson exited the room.

As he appeared outside, Grayson was greeted by Emily running toward him at full speed. He crouched down and scooped her up, letting her sit up on his new, metallic shoulder.

"Wow, Daddy! Your arm got bigger!"

"Yes, it did, Emily," he forced himself to reply as he fought an overwhelming itchiness in his veins.

"Come on! Sixteen-minutes!" Rio shouted from the open sliding door of the helicopter as the rotor blades silently spun up.

"Where are we going?" Emily asked as she rode on Grayson's shoulder.

"We're gonna go help Mommy save the day," Grayson replied as he neared the helicopter.

"Because she's a superhero?" Emily asked.

"That's right, baby. Because she's a superhero," Grayson answered as he stepped into the helicopter and sat Emily down in a cushy seat.

"Hubert, time to haul ass!" Rio shouted to the pilot as he slammed the sliding door closed and gazed out the window at the blue, early morning sky.

The chopper lifted off, gained altitude, tilted forward, and zoomed toward the faintly visible lights of Capital City as the people of Excelsior prayed below.

Chapter 10

HAVE FAITH

Bryan knelt atop a towering construction crane with his mask in his hand as he surveyed the situation in Capital City. Through the windows of Bio-Yomi Tower a block away, Bryan could faintly make out an excess of armed figures occupying most floors of the building. Glancing below, he saw an overpowering army of Bio-Yomi troops outfitted in black military gear, along with tanks and personnel carriers painted white with red Bio-Yomi decals on their armored exterior panels. Hundreds of soldiers standing in formation filled the courtyard and the streets at the base of Bio-Yomi Tower nearly shoulder-to-shoulder. The streets leading to the Bio-Yomi headquarters of Capital City were patrolled by elite units of soldiers and capped off by roadblocks at each intersection.

He then glanced at surrounding apartments and businesses that were completely boarded up with the lights turned out. A Bio-Yomi helicopter passed by overhead, its spotlight weaving in and out of the streets like a rat in a maze. Bryan sighed, put his mask back on, and jumped off the side of the crane. He pressed his palm and shin against the side of the lofty machine and used his magnetism to safely slide toward the ground.

As he neared ten-feet from the concrete below, he pushed off and landed in front of Faith who was casually leaning against the brick wall of an unfinished building. She nonchalantly crossed her mechanical arms as her sheathed katana gently rested on her hip attached to a thin rope tied around her waist.

"Is it as bad as we thought?" Faith asked as she massaged one of her shoulders with her metallic fingers.

"*Much* worse. Hundreds in full kit… with armored vehicles. Looks like Naito assembled his entire army in one spot to make a show of power to go along with his godhood announcement at sunrise," Bryan responded, voice muffled under his steel Tengu mask.

Faith pushed off from the wall, approached a table at the construction site and pulled a piece of olive-green canvas from underneath a circular saw.

"Good. By morning, we'll send a message to the whole world. At any moment, a handful of good people can dethrone *any* tyrannical entity. No matter what shape they take or what banner they fly. If we fail, then freedom fails. I didn't fight through hell with Grayson and rescue my daughter just to have these feuding tyrants take it all away from me now. And I'm about to prove it," Faith said as she draped the canvas over her body like a poncho.

Pride welled inside of Bryan as he nodded at his daughter and turned to walk down a dark alleyway.

"Time to harvest some hope from the blood of these bastards," Bryan confirmed as he disappeared between two buildings.

Faith pulled the canvas tight around her neck, concealing her identity, as she rounded the corner of the building and walked out onto the street. She looked up at the skyscraping roof of Bio-Yomi Tower as her feet followed the white, dotted lines painted on the asphalt.

"Goddammit, we've got another sleep-walker," a pissed-off Bio-Yomi guard whined from behind a vehicle that was blocking the intersection.

Three annoyed soldiers rounded the beefed-up SUV with rifles slung across their chests and postured toward Faith.

"Alright you fuckin' wino, city's on lockdown. Find a hole to crawl in," the lead guard wearily shouted as if it was the one-hundredth time tonight he'd said it.

The guard raised his HK 416 assault rifle, turned off the safety with his thumb, and released a burst of fire at the asphalt next to Faith, pelting her with rocky chunks.

"Well, so much for flying under the radar..." Faith mumbled under the hood of her makeshift poncho.

She continued walking, unphased, as she removed the canvas and threw it to her side. The canvas was swept away with a gust of wind as the soldier's jaw dropped.

"F-Faith..." he stuttered as Faith wrapped her hand around the hilt of her sheathed sword.

As the lead soldier was paralyzed with fear, another one raised his rifle, only for his arms to fall from his body as a rocketing *whoosh* flew by him. His arms, still gripping the rifle, dropped to the ground as the soldier screamed and his knees buckled. Blood drained from his stubs as Bryan's odachi cut another guard's torso diagonally in half both ways, creating an "X" shaped wound across his chest before the meaty slabs of his body splashed to the ground with a few gallons of falling blood and organs.

Faith neared the lead guard who had reached up to his radio and clicked the button.

"F-Faith is here! She—"

Bryan's odachi sliced up the lead guard's groin, through his chest, and out his skull. As his body peeled into two vertical halves, Faith pushed them apart and walked through. Her eyes followed Bryan's massive sword as it flew through the air to a nearby rooftop where Bryan caught it, stuck it to his back, and leapt to another building.

Faith slid across the hood of the white, Bio-Yomi vehicle blocking the intersection, coming face to face with six more soldiers. The cables in her prosthetic arm flared with a bluish hue, as she performed an expert draw-slash into a soldier's armpit, severing his arm, cutting the shoulder strap on his body armor, and cleanly slicing off his head. With a few more lightning-fast slashes reminiscent of a seasoned ronin, the remaining five guards collapsed to the ground as copious amounts of sopping innards ejected from their bodies.

Faith placed her blade in the crook of her prosthetic arm and wiped it clean, sending sparks across her face from the swift metal-on-metal contact. She sheathed her sword and began to sprint toward the final intersection near Bio-Yomi Tower.

An entire platoon of fifty soldiers rounded the corner, surrounding an advancing tank that crushed the roadblock vehicle as it swiveled and lowered its gun to point at Faith. The soldiers took up firing positions, prone, crouched, and standing with several riding on the tank.

Bryan landed in front of Faith, facing down the army with the penetrating eyes of his fiercely intimidating Tengu mask.

"*Shoot 'em!*" an officer at the back of the group shouted as he raised his own pistol with one hand and began firing.

Bryan closed his eyes, brought his fist to his face, and held up two fingers under his mask's nose. Fifty fully-automatic rifles unleashed volleys of bullets in bursts sounding off like firecrackers resounding through the streets. The tank fired its artillery, the recoil rocking the treads atop the crushed vehicle beneath it.

All of the bullets zipped around Bryan and Faith, shredding the windows of the surrounding buildings and chipping away the asphalt behind them. The tank artillery smashed into Bryan and as it exploded, the fire revealed a wavy, translucent bubble surrounding him and Faith. As the firing slowed down and came to an uneven stop, Bryan observed a soldier in the front of the formation drop an empty magazine from his rifle.

Faith and Bryan rushed toward the dense group of soldiers as they both drew their swords and began cutting through them like scythes through crops. Bits of limbs, strips of flesh, and chunky morsels of meat erupted from the crowd as Bryan and Faith ripped through the platoon, methodically slashing away.

With ten soldiers reduced to screaming piles of leaky pulp, they reached the center of the crowd. The remaining soldiers reloaded their weapons and desperately fired on them, but their bullets ricocheted around the invisible bubble emanating from Bryan, zipping through their comrades on the other side. Twenty of the fifty men had been shot or slashed apart before the tank started to reverse and the platoon began to fall apart and retreat toward the Bio-Yomi courtyard.

Bryan tossed his odachi through the windowed slot at the front of the tank and closed his eyes, whipping the sword around the interior like a blender. Shreds of clothing and splashes of blood spewed out of the window as he called the sword back to his hand through the slot.

Breathing heavily, Faith and Bryan pursued the fleeing soldiers around the corner only to face down an armored personnel carrier speeding toward them, aiming to run them over. From one of the windows of the Bio-Yomi Tower, shattered glass fell to the ground as a soldier presented an AT4 rocket launcher and fired his payload at Bryan with a smokey flash.

Bryan reached out his hand, grabbed the air, and made a throwing motion toward the armored vehicle. With Bryan's guidance, the rocket instead collided with the APC and knocked it onto its side as it careened into a building across the street.

Faith rushed toward the soldiers in the street, some of whom began dropping their empty rifles and pulling out knives and batons while others continued to take intermittent pot shots that skimmed around Bryan's barrier.

A deep *poof* echoed from the rooftop of a nearby building as a powerful projectile collided with Bryan's flank and caused his barrier to falter for a moment. He scanned the buildings and saw the glint of a riflescope on a roof top, followed by several other gleams of light from adjacent surrounding rooftops.

Faith collided with the group of soldiers who attempted to fight her with melee weapons to no avail. As one of them thrust at her with his Ka-Bar knife, she sliced into his knuckles and straight down his arm, carving it in half like a split piece of lumber. She continued mercilessly slicing through the crowd as the bodies left behind her cried and groaned. Bryan began launching his sword like a spear into the snipers overhead, impaling them and tossing their remains over the edge. Their mangled bodies fell into the crowd, covering the foot soldiers with fountains of blood as they forcefully impacted the concrete.

Far above, at the top Bio-Yomi Tower, Hiroya casually leaned over the building and watched the carnage unfold below. To him, as Bryan and Faith decimated the guards below, it looked like rows of dominoes falling as the tiny soldiers were slaughtered. Hiroya's glistening six-pack abs on his lean torso flexed as he rested his foot on the rooftop railing and his long, black hair flowed in the wind. The red glow of his exosuit shimmered across his bronzed, sweaty skin as the reflection of the stars in his glossy, black armor began to fade and turn blue with the sky around him.

"The night has taken its first step toward morning, Father. At this rate, they will reach us before the sun climbs the horizon." Hiroya observed, his reverberating voice carrying through the wind.

Hirohiko Naito clasped his hands behind the back of his grey suit as he stared up at the sky. Closing his eyes, he took a deep breath of the fresh air from above the city and held it for a moment before opening his eyes.

"Son, make her pay for what she did to your sister. Go down there... and finish her. She has proven too persistent for a slow death," Naito commanded, giving his son the permission he sought.

Hiroya removed his foot from the railing and lowered it to the ground with a heavy *clank*. He turned and bowed to his father; the joints in his exosuit mechanically whined as they flexed.

"Thank you, Father. I will deliver my vengeance with a ferocity worthy of Kim's memory," he promised as he turned and took a step toward the edge of the roof.

"If you fail me, like you *usually* do, I'll be here to clean up your mess. When Kimberly was savagely killed, I couldn't help but feel like it happened to the wrong child. Let's see if you can change my mind," Mr. Naito mentioned as he rubbed the side of a nine-foot-tall, cube-like container with a shiny, black carbon fiber finish. Red Torii gates glowed on every side of the cube.

Hiroya froze and stared at the ground with wavering eyes for a moment. With teeth clenched, he balled his fist, looked to the edge of the building, and took three swift strides before leaping out of sight.

Hirohiko Naito puffed air from his nose as he turned away to watch the full moon gracefully fall in the distance.

At street-level, Faith and Bryan pressed their backs together as they swung and sliced at the soldiers surrounding them. Suddenly, Hiroya impacted the ground in a crouching stance in front of Faith, crushing the bodies of two soldiers beneath his exosuit's feet. The soldier's bodies popped like bloody tubes of toothpaste as Hiroya slowly straightened his legs and the hydraulics on his joints emitted steam.

All of the soldiers froze in place as Hiroya's menacing, silent presence sucked the life from the battle. Surrounding officers waved their hands downward ordering a cease fire as the red glow of the tubes emanating from the armored device on Hiroya's chest pulsed with his heartbeat. He deliberately walked toward Faith and Bryan, his footsteps *thumping* with every step.

"It appears we may get that duel after all, Faith. When my father had Dr. Borka attempt to recreate the biomagnetic energy source to create a new Steel Fist for his army... I volunteered to be the test subject," Hiroya explained, clanking his fist against the red energy source under the armored device in between his pecs, "This is the moment that determines whether or not Borka was successful."

As Hiroya's voice grew angrier, red electrical jolts popped across his chest. Bryan instinctively put his arm in front of Faith, protectively pushing her back.

"Faith, you killed my *sister*. The only person who *ever loved me. The only person who ever showed me compassion. She* pushed me forward when I couldn't take the pressure of being a Naito *any more*. You killed the only person in my life that I was willing to live for… And now in exchange for her life, I will be taking yours," Hiroya announced righteously as he approached and stopped six-feet shy of Faith.

Faith's chest heaved with breathlessness as she wiped a layer of blood from her face with her mechanical forearm.

"For months, the memory of killing your sister haunted me. I let it rob me of my peace and my strength. I thought no one deserved to die as horrifically as she did. But if your sister wasn't such a batshit crazy, kidnapping, *cunt*… Maybe she wouldn't have had to die. But instead, she wanted to use *my daughter* to take over the world, robbing *billions* of people of their freedom. Now that I've had time to *really* think it over… I wish I could fucking kill her *again*. Anyone who tries to hurt the people I love… They're going to die… *Painfully*," Faith shouted while staring up into Hiroya's face.

Hiroya cracked a heated smile as he fought off a reflexive laugh and broke his eye contact with Faith.

"*You* hurt the person that *I* loved! So… according to *your* logic, what do you expect *me* to do in this moment?!" Hiroya screamed, spitting as he said it.

"Then come and fucking get it, Naito Jr. I'm gonna spank you like I did your sister, then I'm going to buttfuck your daddy with my sword and put an end to Bio-Yomi's squeeze on the world for good," Faith spat back with cool aggression as she shrugged her father's arm off of her.

"Soldiers of Bio-Yomi! Gather around... and witness the *true power* of the Naito family!" Hiroya furiously ordered the surrounding soldiers.

He released a ferocious scream as the right hand of his exosuit opened, catching a massive laser-edged machete that unfolded and launched from his forearm. He rushed at Faith and swung the huge weapon toward her, leaving behind a red streak in the wake of the swing.

With a single hand on her katana, Faith deflected the blow and moved her head an inch to the right, narrowly but effortlessly avoiding injury from the attack.

Clenching his teeth, he opened the other hand of his exosuit and launched a second cyber-machete from his forearm, catching it once more.

"DIE, DIE, DIE, DIE, DIE!" Hiroya cried with each swing as he began to hammer both weapons down on Faith while quickly building up speed.

She and Bryan, walking backwards, began dodging and deflecting the onslaught of attacks from Hiroya as his misses thundered into the ground, spraying fountains of asphalt from each chaotic impact.

Faith deflected an attack from Hiroya's left arm and sliced the wrist of his armored limb to no effect. Bryan, too busy deflecting a flurry of blows from Hiroya to manipulate his sword with his magnetic abilities, raised his arm to block the machetes using his powers, but the weapons and the exosuit were unaffected by his ability to control metal.

Bryan took over deflecting both machetes with his equally-sized odachi as Faith ducked between Hiroya's legs and began slashing the back of his armored body. Two more enormous red-edged machetes, attached to titanium hydraulic arms, folded out from Hiroya's shoulder blades and began whipping at Faith like striking snakes.

"I'll kill you *both* for what you did to her!" Hiroya shrieked as the blinding speed of his attacks continued to increase.

"Dad... I can't... Keep up..." Faith shouted from the other side of Hiroya.

"Yes, you can! Focus!" Bryan firmly instructed as if he were coaching her at a competition.

Two additional laser-machetes folded out from Hiroya's thighs and began thrusting and slashing at Bryan as he dodged and deflected the four weapons. Another two machetes folded out from Hiroya's lower back, striking at Faith.

A blade connected with Bryan's face, ripping the metal Tengu mask away, and revealing the worried exertion on his face. His heavy mask clattered to the ground with a molten gash across the cheek.

"Faith! *Focus!*" Bryan shouted once more. A wave of warm confidence washed over Hiroya's face as he gained the upper hand.

The attacks seemed to slow down for Faith as her vision flickered and she found herself in her father's dojo. She was in full kendo gear and was sparring with her father on the mat.

"Faith, *focus!*" her father shouted before rapidly striking with his bamboo sword.

Her vision pulsed and her consciousness shot back to reality where she was ducking under and dodging the attacks from the four weapons with ease.

Two more machetes folded out in the front and the back of Hiroya's shins and calves as Bryan and Faith dodged six blades each. Beads of sweat dripped from Hiroya's hairline as he expelled pure hatred through his attacks. He leaned back and forth at the hips as he attacked forwards and backwards. As he wildly swung the heavy blades around trying to hit Bryan and Faith, he began to hit surrounding Bio-Yomi soldiers, slicing them in half and sending them flying. The nearby soldiers began to scramble away, unsure of what to do, as they felt the passing heat from the wild blades begin to cook their faces.

Machetes folded out from on top of Hiroya's shoulders, from his ribcage, and from his toes and heels. With twenty-four blades whipping around, Faith and Bryan both stepped away from Hiroya as he extended all of his blades out to his side and fanned them out around his body like peacock feathers.

"A perfect *offense*. A perfect *defense*. I *am* the perfect weapon!" Hiroya's reverberating voice declared as he laughed maniacally into the deep-blue sky that grew brighter by the second.

Bryan punched his hand forward, launching his odachi like a spear at Hiroya's exposed chest. Hiroya swept the blade attached to his right thigh upward, impacting the tip of the odachi causing it to spin in mid-air. With a shout, Hiroya perfectly timed a hit on the pommel of the odachi with a blade from his ribcage, launching it back toward Bryan.

Bryan held out an open hand to stop it, but the odachi's speed was too fast for him to catch. His own sword pierced into his chest and the velocity of the impact sent him flying into the driver-side door of a Bio-Yomi vehicle, denting the red Torii gate decal on the side. Bryan tried and failed to get up before noticing that his odachi had pinned him to the car.

"*Dad—*" Faith shrieked as she ran around Hiroya and toward her father.

Hiroya smacked Faith in the back of her head with the flat side of the blade in his left hand, sending her crashing to the ground.

"Finish him while he's down! *Fire!*" Hiroya ordered the surrounding soldiers as he pointed one of his blades in Bryan's direction.

"*Dad, please!*" Faith pleaded as she lay on the ground, stunned.

Suddenly a roar of engines shook the ground as armored Psychophants vehicles crashed into the Bio-Yomi vehicles blocking the road, sending them airborne into the sea of Bio-Yomi soldiers. Two, then, six, then twelve shoddily painted vehicles retrofitted with parts from bulldozers and snowplows stormed into the crowd as Psychophants members fired fully-automatic firearms and shotguns from slots in the armored windows. A chaotic firefight ensued as Bio-Yomi tanks began firing artillery at the endless wall of vehicles driving through the army of soldiers. Smoking bodies and crumpled car parts scattered across the swarm of soldiers as explosive shockwaves rippled across the city street, causing shards of glass from the surrounding buildings to rain down upon them.

An armored Psychophant pick-up truck launched off of a Bio-Yomi vehicle and careened toward Hiroya. He readied his blades like praying mantis legs and sliced the vehicle apart so swiftly with his twenty-four blades that only scrap metal rained down on him. As a cacophony of gunfire and explosions rang out around him from the battle between the Bio-Yomi soldiers and the invading Psychophants, Hiroya folded the blade in his right hand back into his forearm.

The mechanical spinal column fused to his back split open one vertebra at a time. From his open spine, a mechanical arm deftly presented Faith's biomagnetic sword, Onibi, over his armored shoulder. Hiroya grasped the handle with his hand as the mechanical arm released it and retreated back into his spine before it closed back up with a series of *clinks*.

"And now, Faith, I will kill you just like you killed *her*! I watched you kill her on video thousands of times! It's the only thing that kept me going through the pain of becoming... *this*. I know *exactly* how you did it... Now you will know the *pain* you caused me!" Hiroya vociferated, his heartbeat nearly audible.

He clamped the lever on the handle, igniting the blade in a vibrant, azure flame. Faith rolled over on her back and gazed at her father, weakly trying to remove the sword from his chest.

Hiroya folded all of his blades back into his body and approached Faith with Onibi pointing at her.

"Yes..." he growled with ecstasy, *"Come on Faith... SCREAM!"*

Faith remained silent as Hiroya edged the blinding blade toward her face. She winced as the molten flame of the sword kissed her skin as if she had stuck her head in a furnace.

Beep... Beep... Beep... Beep... Beep...

A van backed up behind Faith and the rear doors shot open.

"Not so fast, Bio-Yomi bitch!" Kurt bellowed as he held a gargantuan Anzio 20mm mag-fed anti-tank rifle at his hip in the back of the van.

He squeezed the trigger and the eight-foot-long rifle recoiled so hard that he lost his grip on it and the buttstock fell to the floor. A cerulean-blue muzzle blast bulged out the walls of the van as a cobalt streak zipped at light speed toward Hiroya.

Reacting to seeing the rifle, Hiroya had extended a blade from his ribcage and braced it with his left arm to use as a shield.

The bullet punched a flaming hole clean through the blade, traveled completely through the arm of the exosuit, exploded out the back, and utterly demolished the structure of the armor. The round continued into the distance with a blue streak until it disappeared into the sky with a white twinkle.

Hiroya's right hand released Onibi, causing it to extinguish and fall to the ground. Faith scrambled over to it, retrieved it, and ran over to her father.

"NO! NOO! *NOOOOO!*" Hiroya shrieked as he fought the controls of his exosuit.

He tried to step forward but the left leg collapsed to its knee and sparked. The left arm began to melt away, so Hiroya pulled his real arm loose from it only to let it dangle and drip melting skin onto the crumbling asphalt. The exosuit was completely frozen in place as small electrical fires began to ignite all over.

"Dad!" Faith shouted as she slid across the ground toward her father and set Onibi down next to him.

She placed her prosthetic foot on the car door and dented it in as she pulled the sword out of his chest. Instead of blood, what looked like gray sand fell from his wound. She helped him up to his feet as he regained his bearings.

There was a hole clean through Bryan's chest, but he did not show even a hint of pain.

"Faith! Thirty-minutes! Let's *go!*" Kurt called out as he motioned toward the capsule in the back of the van that housed the Izanami battle suit.

Bryan tried to conceal the wound in his chest with his damaged armor as he nodded to Kurt.

"I wondered if you were still roaming around," Kurt said as he gave Bryan a jolly smile and laughed.

Faith grabbed Onibi and left behind a trail of dust as she sprinted toward the van. She took Kurt's hand, allowing him to help her in.

At that moment, the brakes of a semi-truck squealed to a halt just past Kurt's van as the air in the brakes hissed. The driver's door of the cab opened and Luden hopped out with two hulking M60E4 machine guns hanging from straps on his shoulders and belts of ammunition running from the guns to two backpacks crisscrossed on his back.

"Damn, Faith! Glad to see you're okay! We'll keep 'em off your ass, but that building's a fucking problem," Luden said as he pointed at gunfire raining down on the Psychophants from Bio-Yomi Tower. "Think you can help us out on the way to your meeting with Naito?"

Faith flashed Luden a smile and nodded as a few bullets whizzed past him and peppered the cab of the semi-truck.

"I'll see what I can do," she replied, hiding a cocky smile.

"Grayson's on his way. If you can hold out until he gets here, there's a small chance we could actually win this thing," Luden added.

An army of Psychophants with makeshift spiked shields, clubs, and an assortment of firearms gathered behind Luden.

"Psychophants! For *EXCELSIOR!*" Luden roared as he raised one fist to the sky before slamming Brazier's armor prism into his chest.

"*EXCELSIOR!*" the Psychophants echoed in unison.

The black, scaled armor released itself from the prism, completely covering Luden's body as he leveraged the two M60E4s under his arms and charged into the bloody sea of Bio-Yomi soldiers and Psychophants. Slice slid into the driver's seat of the armored-up semi-truck, shifted into low gear and drove into the crowd, supplying moving cover for his compatriots.

In the back of the van, Kurt pressed a button on the capsule containing Project Izanami, causing the reflective windowed shield to retract.

"I prepped it before I left, but you'll still have to pair to it. Just like last time, it'll hurt like a bitch and we'll have to surgically remove the damn thing from you. The five-minute timer on the energy source starts the second pairing is complete. The energy source will heal your wounds so you'll be unkillable as long as the suit remains intact and powered on," Kurt informed her as he double checked cords and wires stretching from the suit's container into several jury-rigged Bio-Yomi battery stations.

Faith held up her prosthetic hand and showed him the ring with an inset energy source. Kurt tilted his head up to look through his bifocals and raised his white, bushy eyebrows.

"Well, that oughta extend your time a bit… But there's no telling by how long… Grayson will be cutting it real close, and I'm afraid Naito might bolt if we get too close to overrunning him. He won't want to look like a loser in front of everyone. The output on this capsule is low, so it'll take ten minutes to pair you. We need to start *now*, if you ask me," Kurt explained, his soothing voice faltering a bit from the adrenaline.

Faith stared at the capsule for a moment, reliving the pain from the first time she paired with it. She took a deep breath, climbed into the capsule, and laid in the open Izanami suit. The windowed shield closed over her and steam shot into the capsule. The monitor next to the capsule read: "Project Izanami Pairing 0%"

As the spikes on the spine of the suit punctured her back, she flinched and her vision went dark.

CHAPTER 11
THE FINAL COUNTDOWN

"*FAITH!*" Hiroya wailed as he ripped the red tubes attached to his chest out of the exosuit and fell to the ground.

He stood up, the red, swirling energy source in his chest dimly fading. Clear tubes attached to his torso dragged behind him as he staggered toward the van.

Bryan stepped in front of him, dragging the blade of his odachi across the ground.

Hiroya stared at Faith in the capsule through the hole in Bryan's chest.

"*Out of my WAY! I HAVE to KILL HER!*" Hiroya screeched in desperation.

"And *I'm* in your way. Let's see what you're made of… *Hiroya Naito,*" Bryan said as he lifted his odachi from the ground and held it at the ready.

Hiroya turned around, grabbed the blade with the bullet hole in it, and ripped his exosuit's hand from the handle. The blade no longer had an illuminated, laser edge, but a wedged edge with chips in it.

Bryan watched Hiroya's toned muscles flex as he lifted the large blade to a fighting position. Hiroya released a gravelly exhale as he summoned every last bit of energy he had left.

After a slight pause, they stared each other down as a harmony of gunfire erupted around them. Twisting their feet into the asphalt, they both swung simultaneously.

With a violent *clang*, the massive blades impacted each other on their edges, and recoiled back from the force. They continued to slowly heave the oversized blades at each other from different angles as sparks ignited with each impact.

Zooming past the clashing blades, Luden hurdled over piles of dead bodies as soldiers, both friend and foe, collapsed around him. Maneuvering through the chaotic melee, he hopped from car to car, denting the roofs, as he made his way toward the entrance of Bio-Yomi Tower.

A group of one hundred Bio-Yomi soldiers had taken cover and dug in to the courtyard of the Bio-Yomi Building. Luden approached the courtyard as his soldiers clashed with the stragglers in the street. An artillery shell from a tank collided with Luden, completely immolating his armor, but leaving him unscathed. On fire and armored, he entered the courtyard by himself and hip fired his machine guns while shrugging off bullets with ease. Luden's flaming armor reflected the deafening muzzle flashes of his bulky rifles as he couldn't help but smile a toothy grin under the scaled helmet of his suit.

The flames on Luden's suit extinguished as a Bio-Yomi helicopter crashed nearby, sending a shockwave toward the courtyard. A group of Psychophants cheered at the destroyed helicopter until gunfire from the upper floor of the tower connected with a few of them, sending them running back to the semi-truck for cover.

Bio-Yomi soldiers were completely shredded by Luden's machine gun fire as he methodically looked behind every piece of cover and mercilessly eliminated them one-by-one. As he approached the final enemy, a Bio-Yomi officer wearing a beret, the officer fired his CZ-85 Combat handgun in his direction. The bullets sparked and ricocheted off of Luden's scaley armor until it ran dry and the officer frightenedly tossed it to the ground.

The officer fell to his knees and clasped his hands with tears rolling down his cheeks as Luden, covered head to toe in obsidian armor, walked toward him.

"P-Please! I have a family! We were just following orders!" the officer begged.

"Just following orders? The invulnerable psychopath on the roof wouldn't even exist if it weren't for men like you who just followed orders. Let me wash the taste of leather out of your mouth, you boot-licking insect," Luden coldly replied, his voice muffled under his armored suit.

Luden held down the triggers of his M60E4s as a rush of 7.62mm bullets erupted from the smoking barrels, shell casings flew from the chamber, and pieces of bullet-links jingled to the ground. The officer convulsed as the bullets ripped through every inch of his body leaving behind shredded, fleshy holes in their wake. His body fell to the ground, unrecognizable and seeping.

A bullet skipped off of Luden's head from above and impacted the ground next to him. He looked up at several soldiers shooting at him from the third-floor window. Holding down the triggers of his machine guns, he shredded the glass of the second and third floor windows, impacting the shooters and causing them to plummet to the ground.

Noticing his guns were empty, he shrugged off the ammo backpacks and tossed the belt-fed machine guns at his feet.

"Faith... Where are you..." Luden asked aloud as he glanced down the street.

In the van, Kurt glimpsed over his shoulder at the duel between Hiroya and Bryan as the monitor read: "Project Izanami Pairing 99% complete." Kurt looked at his watch and bit the inside of his cheek as the second hand shifted the time to 5:45.

Bryan and Hiroya struggled against one another in a complete deadlock. Hiroya dropped the tip of his blade to the ground, breathing heavily and dragging it across the pulverized street. The silvery skin on Bryan's neck started to crack and crumble away.

"Looks like your time's about up. You are a *dead man walking*," Hiroya snarled, huffing and puffing.

"So are you," Bryan replied, pointing to the red power source in Hiroya's chest flickering and fading.

A *ding* reminiscent of an analogue microwave sounded off from the inside of the van. Kurt watched as the monitor read: "Project Izanami Pairing Complete."

Steam erupted from the capsule as the windowed shield retracted. A metal backing rose up and presented Faith in the Izanami suit like an ejected cassette tape.

A sleek black helmet with a golden visor over Faith's eyes was attached to a slim-fitting, black, skeletal exosuit that covered her shoulders, arms, spine, hips and legs. A vented, triangular, turbine engine rested on the upper back of the armor and razor-sharp, curved claws extended from her knuckles.

Faith opened her eyes, seeing everything in thermal vision with auto-targeting, just as she remembered. She turned her head to look at Kurt.

"Fifteen-minutes, killer. Go get him," Kurt said with a confident nod, handing her Onibi.

She wrapped her metal fingers around the sword's hilt, ignited the turbine engine on her back, and exploded out of the van, shattering the cracked windshield with the backblast. The Psychophants down below cheered and pointed as she soared over their heads and crashed through a second-floor window of Bio-Yomi Tower.

"Well, I've done all I can do. It's in your hands, now," Luden said under his breath as he pried a rifle out of a dead man's hand and joined the Psychophants in firing on the remaining Bio-Yomi soldiers.

Faith ripped through floor after floor, crashing through ceilings and shattering windows with the explosive flames from her Onibi sword. Bio-Yomi soldiers unleashed blood-curdling screams and horrifically melted away into mucky ash with each slice of her blade.

The Psychophants on the street below overran the last of the Bio-Yomi troops as Faith darted through the tower, igniting each level in seconds. Flashes of blue light strobed across each floor as she ripped through the building like a killer hummingbird, murdering waves of Bio-Yomi troops in her path. Reaching the top floor, she slashed through two soldiers who were reloading shoulder-fired missiles, causing their bodies to burn from the inside out. As their blue ashes drifted away, she crashed out the window and boosted up to the rooftop, landing fifty-feet away from Hirohiko Naito.

Faith lifted the feet of her Izanami suit out of the crumbling concrete beneath her as she surveyed the rooftop, noticing the sizable carbon-fiber cube behind Naito.

"I suppose I should not be surprised that the woman who could best my daughter made it all the way here," Naito commended her, glancing at his Rolex and chuckling to himself.

Faith ignited Onibi, its brilliant blue flame reflecting off of her golden visor. Naito grinned at her futile attempt to intimidate him.

"You know, I... *convinced*... Borka to reveal that he was hiding away the cloning data of the parasite. *I convinced* him to fill in the gaps and recreate the parasite. *I convinced* him to implant the parasite directly into my body. Then, *I convinced* him to truly destroy the data for good. So that *I* would be the only one with this... *power*. But do you know who convinced *me* to do all of that?" Naito asked as he paced back and forth, his dress shoes tapping the concrete roof.

"Stop stalling, you piece of shit," Faith threatened forcefully.

"Or what?" Naito asked, "You and I both know you can't kill me. I know your little suit is on the clock... but it's of no use regardless."

Faith adjusted her grip on Onibi as she looked around in the projected three-hundred-and-sixty-degree view of her visor, hoping to see a sign of Grayson.

"As I was saying... *you* convinced me to do this. When I was first seeking immortality, it was to evolve mankind. I could select individuals fit to be world leaders and I could create an everlasting world order. I could choose visionary scientists, and grant them as many years as they needed to complete their research. I could have *truly* changed the world. But when you *murdered* my daughter... that all disappeared. I adopted *her* aspirations. I saw the wisdom hidden away in her immaturity. If *I* was the only person with eternal life... Then *I* could *control* the world. Instead of evolving it, I could take the helm. Steer anyone in any direction I wanted. I realized that true power isn't shared. True power is having complete, absolute, undivided *control.* And the best way to obtain this control—" Naito continued.

"Is fear..." Faith interrupted, finishing his sentence.

"Exactly. And who isn't afraid of an indestructible man? A god among mortals?" Naito bragged with a crooked smile.

"*Me,*" Faith responded with unwavering confidence.

"You see, Faith, that's exactly why I'm glad you're here. I was originally going to perform a different demonstration of my abilities… But I didn't get to where I am without recognizing opportunities and seizing them without hesitation. In seven minutes, a live satellite broadcast will appear on every television, computer, and smart device in the world. And on that broadcast, I will be killing *you* for all to see," Naito said, reaching into his pocket and removing a small remote.

Naito pressed a button on the remote and all of the bolts on the massive Bio-Yomi crate next to him exploded, causing the walls of the cube to fall open. Resting in place of the crate was a large, white, four-legged, spider-like robot with a silver harness in the middle. Branching off from the harness were two .50 caliber turrets, missile launchers, grenade launchers, and two scythe-shaped blades.

"Even though you can't kill me, I certainly wouldn't be able to kill *you*, either," Naito said as he approached the harness of the cyber-abomination, "But with *this*, I will rip that suit from your body and peel your skin off with it for what you did to my Kimberly."

Naito backed up against the harness as spikes shot out from it, piercing his back, shoulders, and arms. A helmet with a red visor lowered over his eyes as a screw drilled into the top of his head and into his brain. The robot came to life and the spider-legs stood up straight as Naito's legs dangled above the ground. Naito's terrifying silhouette rested against the morning sky as it slowly turned orange.

"Time to soften you up before the big show," Naito trumpeted as the weapons locked on to Faith.

The booster on Faith's back erupted as she skated across the roof. Naito laughed as he fired the .50 caliber turrets at Faith, the bullets impacting the ground behind her before catching up and hitting her directly.

Faith fell to the ground as her body was pulverized by the large-caliber rounds. She held up her arms to shield herself from the bullets as the energy source glowed on her back, healing her substantial wounds.

She frantically boosted again flying straight up past the large, red, neon Torii gate that topped off Bio-Yomi Tower. The bullets from Naito's weapons shredded the sign as sparks erupted from it and it teetered off the roof, falling down below. It collided with the side of the tower before bouncing off and violently crashing into the street. A wall of rising dust floated into the air as if a building had just been demolished.

Killing her engine, she fell back to the roof and boosted directly toward Naito. With Onibi ignited, she slashed at one of the spider-like legs, but her sword rebounded off of it.

"This weapon was designed out of my *fear* of having to face you. You *cannot* beat it!" Naito boasted through a soft smile.

One of the mantis-like blades sliced through Faith's torso, chopping her in half, and impacting the spine of her suit, sending her flying into the rooftop-access door and down a flight of stairs. She grunted in pain as the suit's energy source painfully healed and reconnected her body.

Naito unleashed a barrage of rockets and grenades at the walled-in rooftop access area, completely blowing it to smithereens.

"Five minutes, Faith! Feeling warmed up, yet?" Naito crowed into the rising dust and smoke.

"If I tell him the Government is launching a nuke at him in five minutes, he might run. I need to hold him here at all costs. Besides, this is where Grayson is headed... If Naito moves, we're all dead," Faith thought to herself as her mind ran blank.

Faith exploded from underneath the rubble and zoomed through the smoke causing it to swirl behind her as she ignited her sword and prepared to attack once more.

At street-level, Bryan cleaved his chipped and cracked odachi's blade into Hiroya's muscular shoulder, burying the heavy sword deep into his chest. Hiroya dropped his huge machete to the ground and fell to his knees. The edge of the sun teased the horizon behind Hiroya as his head drooped toward his chest.

"Father… is going… to hate me…" he mumbled before the red energy source in his chest went dark.

Bryan breathed heavily as another chalky, silvery chunk fell from his cheek.

"You were a good fighter, son. Maybe you'll find a better family in the next life," Bryan said as he pulled his sword from Hiroya's body, letting him limply crash to the ground.

Kurt walked up to Bryan and placed a hand on his shoulder.

"I'm glad I got to see you today, old friend," Kurt sentimentally expressed as Bryan turned around.

Bryan stood tall, silently fighting through overwhelming exhaustion.

"Kurt… While I can… I'd like to say thank you. For protecting my daughter. I—" Bryan gratefully recited as he searched for the right words.

A sad smile took over Kurt's face as he pulled Bryan in for a hug.

"Think nothing of it, my friend," Kurt said, patting Bryan's back.

Kurt lightly pushed away from the hug, but kept his hands on Bryan's shoulders.

"Now you're back, and it's your turn to protect your daughter again," Kurt said as he glanced up to the roof of Bio-Yomi Tower, "Get up there, Bryan. She needs her father."

Bryan placed his hand on Kurt's shoulder once more and squeezed it with a nostalgic smile.

They both looked into the auburn sky as Rio's Government helicopter passed overhead, soaring toward the peak of the building.

"See you on the other side, Kurt," Bryan said, releasing Kurt's shoulder.

Kurt nodded and wiped a tear from his cheek bone as Bryan ran toward the building and began to sprint vertically up the side of it, leaping from one piece of exposed metal to another.

In the sky, Rio opened the sliding door of the helicopter as he checked his watch.

"Jesus... Three minutes..." he agonized, feeling his heart thumping in his chest.

The wind from the outside sucked away his crocodile cowboy hat, but he was so focused on the time that he didn't notice.

Emily pointed out the window of the chopper as they approached the rooftop. Faith continued to dodge around Naito, slashing his body whenever she saw an opening.

"Look, Daddy! Mommy's fighting a monster! Because she's a superhero, right?"

"That's right, Emily. Your Mom is one hell of a superhero," he responded with a smile of relief that she was still alive.

Grayson approached the open door of the chopper and clamped his steel fist on the edge of it.

"Are you a superhero, too, Daddy?" Emily asked.

"We're about to find out, Honey," Grayson answered as he bent his knees preparing to jump.

"Get us *close*, dammit!" Rio shouted at the pilot as his hands visibly shook.

The helicopter initiated a low flyover of the rooftop as Grayson smiled at Emily.

"I love you, Emily," he said tenderly before he leapt from the helicopter.

As the chopper flew past the roof, Emily waved out the window.

"I love you, too, Daddy!" she yelled, pushing against her seatbelt as the chopper pulled back from the roof and began to circle.

Chapter 12
WIN OR LOSE

Grayson impacted the roof, absorbing the fall with his steel fist, causing the cement to crack in a spiderweb pattern. As he quickly got his bearings, he saw an explosion ignite from Naito as Faith flew backwards and crashed into the ground next to him.

"Faith, we've—"

Faith quickly jumped to her feet and ran toward Naito as she dodged a string of oncoming bullets.

"No time! Helmet off!" she shouted as she boosted across the ground, darted around Naito, and slashed his last remaining .50 caliber turret in half.

Grayson looked at Naito's horrifying spider-like mech and saw the helmet pierced into his skull. He closed some distance, drew the .500 magnum from behind his right hip, cocked the hammer, and fired a shot as Faith continued to distract Naito.

The powerful hardcast bullet dented the helmet and forced the spider-like mechanical legs to falter.

"Grayson, so glad you could join!" Naito shouted as his body dangled from the helmet.

All of Naito's weapons, except for his mantis blades, were scattered across the ground in pieces, slowly melting away with blue fire.

Naito knocked Faith away with one of his blades and scurried toward Grayson. With seconds to react, Grayson pulled the double action trigger of his revolver while staring at the front sight covering Naito's head.

The cylinder cycled and the hammer fell on the firing pin as a fiery explosion mushroomed from the snub-nose barrel. As the roaring bullet connected between Naito's eyes, his head momentarily exploded into a liquified mess. At the same time, Faith boosted in, grabbed Naito's body and ripped it off of the spikes on the harness.

The inertia of the robotic weapon's movement sent it tumbling off the edge of the building as Faith tossed Naito's body aside. Naito's decapitated figure stood up and brushed himself off as his head promptly reformed. He checked his watch and adjusted the cufflinks on his burned and slashed suit.

"Nearly one minute until the broadcast. I suppose I'll just stand here and let you attack me for the camera. That should prove to the world that I am *eternal*," Naito said with satisfaction.

From the sky, Bryan's odachi pierced diagonally through Naito's left shoulder, exited his groin, and punched deep into the concrete, pinning him to the roof like a scarecrow.

As Naito's weight limply hung forward against the sword, Grayson closed the fingers on his steel fist pinky-to thumb, clanking them one-by-one against his palm. He whipped the arm back as if to punch and the fist began to charge up. The knuckles retracted against the forearm, the hydraulic pistons compressed, and the flexible metal on the bicep began to swell.

In the helicopter above, Rio held a radio in his shaking hand as he watched the seconds count down on his watch.

Naito grabbed the sword and started to push into the edge, forcing it to cut further through him. He managed to shimmy halfway off the sword as Grayson's bicep started to faintly glow blue.

"Grayson, do it!" Faith yelled.

The blade began to cut through Naito's back as he struggled against the sword, nearly free.

"It's not… not yet," Grayson stuttered helplessly.

As Faith crouched to ignite her booster, Bryan walked up behind Naito, wrapped his arms around his torso and pulled him back into the sword.

"What, who—" Naito started to say as he glanced back and recognized Bryan's face.

Naito's eyes snapped back to Grayson whose large, metallic arm violently shook with raw power.

"I love you, Cherry Blossom," Bryan peacefully said to Faith.

Faith fell to one knee with tears streaming down her dirty cheeks before she swallowed her tears and simply nodded.

"I love you, too, Dad."

Grayson gritted his teeth and screamed as he released his charged punch with all of his might.

For a moment, the world was sucked toward Grayson, before a blinding flash ignited in front of him. The knuckles of the fist and the hydraulic piston extended, shattering every bone in Naito's face. An unfathomable blast of energy exploded from the punch releasing a conical wave that traveled a mile across the sky, dissolving the clouds above. The concrete beneath Naito vaporized, carving out twelve stories of the building beneath him like a slice of cake as structures in line with the punch began to collapse into clouds of dust in the distance. The vent flaps in the biceps opened, expelling steam as a thick cloud of smoke and dust rose from the roof.

In the helicopter, Rio's thumb hovered over the button on the radio as he waited for the smoke to clear.

"Come on… *come on…*" he chanted as the second hand on his watch was twenty seconds from the hour.

Grayson turned his steaming fist over and saw bright blue lights peeking through cracks of the decaying biomagnetic energy fragment.

Faith boosted up and out of a pile of rubble, landed back on the roof, and looked over at Grayson whose arm started to violently shake.

"Gray?" Faith asked, confused by what was happening.

"Faith, get out of here!" he said, holding up his right hand.

Without hesitation, Faith boosted over to Grayson, ignited Onibi and sliced off the steel fist above the fragment. She wrapped her arms around him, kicked off the ground, and boosted off of the roof. The fist fell ten stories before it detonated beneath them.

The blast cleared enough smoke from the roof for Rio to see clearly. Naito had been completely disintegrated. He slammed his finger down on the button of the radio and spoke faster than he knew he could.

"Bravo-charlie-alpha-alpha-delta-romeo-zero-niner-niner, cancel launch, over," he said, petrified, as he helplessly witnessed the hands on his watch move to 6:00.

With Grayson in her arms, Faith crashed through what was left of a window in an adjacent building. As they skidded to a stop on the floor, the energy source on the Izanami suit turned gray, and powered down.

Rio froze in place, despondently staring at his watch as nothing but silence came through the radio.

"Roger that, launch cancelled," a voice called out over the radio.

Rio slumped down to the floor of the helicopter and rested an arm on his knee as he watched the sun rise over the horizon, painting Capital City with a golden light.

In the building, Grayson laid on top of Faith with her arms still wrapped around him.

"Are you gonna let me go?" Grayson asked with an awkward smile.

"Remember? When the suit shuts down, it completely locks up. We're stuck here," she answered, giggling at the thought.

"Well, I can think of worse places to be stuck," he said as he closed his eyes, passionately kissed her, then lifted away.

Her golden visor retracted into her helmet as she looked deeply into his vibrant eyes.

"What would I do without you, Grayson?" Faith asked, lost in the moment.

"The same thing I'd do without you…" he replied as his soft lips met hers once more.

Grayson and Faith continued to kiss in a pile of glass as the chopper hovered outside.

Rio turned to face Emily with a look of compassion on his face.

"Listen, I'm sorry about your parents, Kiddo," Rio quietly expressed as Emily looked out the window.

Emily shrugged as she looked over at him.

"It's okay… I know it's gross… but I've seen them do kissing before. They do it because they love each other," Emily said, genuinely explaining kissing to Rio.

Confused, Rio rushed over to her window and saw Grayson and Faith in the adjacent building laying on top of one another.

"You sons of bitches, you pulled it off," he cheered to himself before leaning into the cockpit, "Why don't you take us down, we'll have to get Kurt up there to… uh… separate them."

The helicopter tilted away as the morning light shined into the building and two colorful love birds fluttered past the window by Grayson and Faith.

Epilogue

PEACE AND QUIET

A harmony of controlled gunfire echoed into the afternoon sky above the desert oasis of Excelsior.

"All right! Cease fire and set them down!" Grayson yelled as he raised his prosthetic arm into the air.

A line of a dozen young, adolescent boys and girls obediently rested their handguns on the tables in front of them. A light cloud of dust rose from the dirt berm behind a series of hand-drawn silhouette targets with angry faces.

"Excellent shooting, everyone! Stephanie, you've *really* improved, great job!" Grayson complimented as he walked behind the row of youthful shooters.

Grayson leaned over and reached into a backpack, retrieving a large watermelon.

"I told you guys I'd have a surprise for you today. Come on!" he said, beckoning them to follow as he approached the target area.

The kids excitedly tailed Grayson as he set the watermelon on a table and took a few steps back.

"Bombs away!" Grayson hollered as he unholstered a Smith and Wesson Model 69 Combat Magnum, skillfully pointed it at the watermelon, and pulled the double action trigger.

The .44 magnum revolver boomed and recoiled in his hand, releasing a puff of smoke, as the watermelon exploded into a misty mess. Chunks of pink fruit flew back and rained down on the group of kids as they giggled and gossiped about how cool it was. Grayson placed the revolver back into his black, leather holster and clapped his hands.

"Okay, kids! That's it for today, so feel free to visit your older friends as they finish up their training," Grayson said as the kids yelled their thanks to Mr. Grayson and took off toward a large, nearby canopy.

Grayson's boots crunched in the dirt as he approached the neighboring area shaded by a makeshift, industrial-sized awning. Short bursts of yelling grew louder as he walked into the shade and placed his arm around Faith's waist.

"How are they doing?" Grayson asked, giving Faith's hip a squeeze just above her mechanical thigh.

"They suck," she replied with her bionic arms crossed as she observed an older teenage boy and girl with wooden swords facing each other down, surrounded by a circle of sitting students.

The two teens hollered and flailed their swords around for a few seconds before the girl struck the boy in the arm with a *thwack*.

"You can do better than that, Kacey! Hit him in the *head*!" Faith yelled like a soccer mom.

"Sorry, sensei!" the girl shouted back before bowing to the injured boy.

"When is Luden going to build a proper dojo around here?" Faith asked angrily as she waved the teens away.

"Looks like someone is turning into her old sensei over here," Grayson teased as he kissed her cheek and pulled her close.

"Good hustle today everyone, but you can all do better. Practice, practice, *practice!*" Faith shouted as her students lined up and bowed to her.

After Faith reciprocated their bow, the teenagers began to strip off their protective gear and gather around a mini-fridge plugged into a generator.

"Mommy! Daddy!" Emily's little voice called from behind them.

Slice crouched down and gently nudged Emily's back as she darted toward her parents. Faith scooped up her daughter and held her close as Grayson ruffled her hair.

"Hey guys! Luden sent us over to tell you he's got a big update. Head on over as soon as you can," Slice said with a smiling nod before waving goodbye to Emily and jogging toward a man struggling to carry an ammo crate.

"Your uncle Luden has been gone for a few days; do you want to go see him with us?" Grayson asked Emily as Faith set her on the ground.

"What do *you* think? Of *course* I do!" Emily sassily replied.

Grayson and Faith raised their eyebrows at each other as Emily spun around, huffed, and walked toward Excelsior's center.

"Less time around Kurt from now on?" Grayson joked.

"Not a chance. It's too adorable," Faith responded with a kindhearted smile as they followed closely behind Emily.

As Emily, Faith, and Grayson entered the ragged, steel structure in the center of Excelsior, they could hear voices rambunctiously conversing in Luden's office. They rounded the corner, entered the room, and saw Luden leaning against his desk with a towering pile of guns atop it. Rio sat on the dusty couch in the room, manspreading his legs, and digging into a crumpled bag of barbecue chips. Kurt's belly jiggled in his chair by the pool table as he neared the end of a hysterical laugh while Borka stiffly grinned next to him in his wheelchair.

"Well, hello there, family!" Kurt said as he removed his glasses and wiped a tear, caused by laughter, from his eye.

Rio grinned while chewing his crunchy chips as he watched Emily dart across the room, crashing into Luden's leg.

Luden recoiled from the impact, scooped Emily up, pushed aside some guns on his desk, and set her down on the edge of it.

"I missed you, Luden!" Emily said, giggling.

"I missed you, too, Emily!" Luden replied politely, patting her head. "Grayson, close that behind you, will ya?"

Grayson sealed shut the heavy, steel door and shoved the locking bar into position with a weighty *clank*.

"Slice told us there was a big update. What's going on?" Faith asked the group as she crossed her arms and leaned against the wall by the door.

"Yeah, you could say that," Rio chimed in as he tilted his head back and poured the remaining crumbs from his chip bag into his mouth, causing a black, leather cowboy hat to fall off his head.

"*Update* is a bit of an understatement... I think this qualifies as *big news*," Kurt added as Grayson sat on a stool next to him.

Luden pushed himself off the desk, approached the pool table in the middle of the room, and casually leaned forward onto it.

"It seems our actions a few weeks ago have set things in motion and you'd better *believe* we are going to seize the day on this one. The chaotic power grab over Bio-Yomi's assets ended in a win for us. The muscle of the Psychophants was able to crush the Bio-Yomi holdouts and convince the stragglers to join us. Borka is going to be returning to Bio-Yomi to head up R&D with the sole purpose of creating a cure for Vax addiction while maintaining a steady rollout of Vax so people don't die in the meantime," Luden explained, addressing the room.

Grayson rested his mechanical hand on Borka's shoulder.

"That's good to hear. You sure you're up for it?" Grayson asked.

Kurt glanced at Faith, then over at Grayson.

"He's definitely up for it. Because I'll be going with him."

Luden pushed his sleeves up to his elbows and sighed.

"I'm giving Bio-Yomi to Kurt. He'll be headed into the adjacent Territory where the next biggest Bio-Yomi facility is located to take over. Kurt'll be working with other countries to ensure Vax continues to ship out while they work on the cure. He's the only person I trust to juggle that kind of power and influence."

Grayson slapped Kurt on the back and squeezed his shoulder.

"I can't think of anyone better," Grayson said with a delighted smile on his face.

Faith courteously smiled and turned her head, attempting to hide her watery eyes.

"Borka and I were actually just hanging around here waiting to say goodbye to you all. There's a caravan waiting for us at the gates. I'm afraid there's no time to lose…" Kurt somberly explained as he stood up from his chair, his prosthetic legs gently humming from the movement.

Grayson rose from his seat and faced Kurt, extending his right hand. Kurt took hold and proudly shook it before pulling him in for a hug.

"You take care of your little girl, now, Grayson," Kurt mumbled into Grayson's shoulder.

"Take care of yourself and keep in touch," Grayson responded through a lump in his throat.

As they pulled apart, Kurt nodded and walked over to Emily at the desk and gave her a grandfatherly bear hug. Grayson looked at Borka who was faintly smiling at him.

"Thanks for everything, Sebastian. It's time to make things right... For everyone who didn't make it," Grayson affirmed with a shaky sparkle in his eye.

"I will make you proud, Grayson. Kurt will be fitting me with prosthetics upon arrival at the facility to make my work a bit easier..." Borka replied to Grayson through an earnest smirk as he rubbed the eyepatch under his glasses with the back of his hand.

Kurt returned, waved goodbye to Emily and took hold of the handles on Borka's wheelchair. Luden and Kurt exchanged nods as he walked toward the door.

Faith, leaning against the wall, reached over and undid the lock bar on the door, pushing it open as she coolly looked ahead.

Kurt approached the doorway with Borka and stopped next to Faith.

"You be sure to come visit every once in a while. I can tune up that suit of yours if you do," Kurt offered with his usual heartfelt smile.

Faith suddenly lost her composure as her face distorted and tears emerged from her eyes. She sobbed as she lunged forward and wrapped her arms around Kurt's neck.

"I know, I know," Kurt said while comforting her and returning the hug with a single arm. "I'm going to make sure you and everyone else in the Territories is taken care of. After all, Bryan is watching us now. We have to make sure to do right by him."

Faith nodded and softly pulled away from Kurt, letting a hand linger on his shoulder as she tried to calm her sobs.

"Thank you for taking care of us," Faith managed to say.

Kurt placed his hand over hers as he tried to fight his own tears.

"My pleasure, Faith," Kurt sincerely replied before squeezing her hand and releasing it.

Faith then crouched down, placed her hand on Borka's, and sorrowfully smiled at him. He returned the smile and gave her a nod of understanding as Kurt wheeled him out of the room and turned the corner out of sight.

Emily crawled down from the desk and trotted over to Faith.

"Mommy, why are you crying?"

Faith pulled her daughter close and stole a hug for her own comfort.

"Because that's the first time I've truly had the chance to say goodbye to someone I care about, sweetie."

Rio rose to his feet from the crumb-riddled couch and hiked up his belt.

"I don't mean to break up the moment here, but Luden and I have some politics and strategy to discuss. The Government is none-too-happy about Luden and Kurt essentially inheriting all of Naito's power, so we have to figure out how to head them off at the pass… so to speak," Rio said as he stepped over an ammo can and approached the pool table where Luden stood.

Luden shuffled around maps, blueprints, and documents on the table as Grayson joined Faith and Emily.

"You guys are welcome to stay in Excelsior for as long as you want. I know the people here appreciate all you've done and continue to do for them. You can consider yourself family to the Psychophants," Luden said as he paused to appreciate the beauty of Grayson, Faith, and Emily united in a moment of peace.

"Thanks, Luden. You know we'll always have your back," Grayson assured him as he picked up Emily, placed his other arm across Faith's shoulders, and ushered them out of the room.

The family approached the humble little abode they called home in Excelsior as the sun began to set. Faith pushed open the door as Grayson revved up the generator outside.

The lights in the single room glowed dim for a few seconds upon entry before properly lighting the interior. The walls of the room were intricately painted with desert skylines, swirling stars, and extravagant vistas.

Emily ran over to her bed and leapt into a pile of pillows on her mattress. Grayson sat down beside her and began playfully attacking her with his prosthetic arm as she picked up a pillow to use as a shield. Painted on the wall by Emily's bed were two coyotes chasing a rabbit through a starry desert landscape.

Faith sauntered past the capsule containing her Izanami suit and made her way over to an easel in the corner of the room. She glanced at her katana and Onibi mounted on the wall next to the capsule before turning her attention toward her workspace.

She removed the olive-colored sheet that covered the easel, sat in her wooden stool, and retrieved her painting pallet from a nearby table. Grasping a paintbrush in her mechanical fingers, she began to skillfully stroke her brush across the canvas. An uplifting smile adorned her face while she listened to Grayson and Emily playing next to her as she applied the finishing touches to her painting of a samurai napping against a cherry blossom tree.

Made in the USA
Las Vegas, NV
25 September 2021